ONE

"We've found another victim."

Lexi Simmons tensed at Sergeant Tomlinson's words flowing through her Bluetooth. *Not again.* She eased to a stop at a red light and gripped the steering wheel more tightly. "Where this time?"

"A couple miles outside Harmony Grove."

Harmony Grove. *Home.* She closed her eyes, dread sifting over her.

Tomlinson continued, "Look, you're from there. You might know the victim. So if you need to be excused from this one, all you've got to do is say the word."

She swallowed back the bile rising in her throat. Criminals who preyed on women were the worst. And Tomlinson was right. She probably *did* know the victim. Harmony Grove was a tiny town.

"No, I'm all right. I can handle it. Give me what you've got."

A horn sounded behind her and she stepped on the gas. She had left Polk County Sheriff's Office five minutes earlier, looking forward to a girls' night out with her cousin Kayla. Dinner and a movie.

Her plans had just changed.

Tomlinson began relaying the details of the case in that impersonal monotone that underscored the subject's status as just another statistic. Each new case was a repeat of the last, five in all. Except this one had occurred in Harmony Grove.

She braked to a stop at the last traffic light before leaving town and disconnected the call. She would phone Kayla, leaving a message if she had to. Kayla would understand. Lexi's job came first. There was a reason she had changed her major from business to law enforcement, and that girl lying in the woods, cold and alone, was it.

Three miles before reaching the outskirts of Harmony Grove, the road ahead disappeared under a flashing display of red and blue. Other law-enforcement officers were already on site, securing the scene, keeping away the curious. So was the Polk County Sheriff's Office crime scene unit.

She slipped between two Harmony Grove Police Department vehicles and ground to a halt. This was the county's jurisdiction, but so close to the city limits that Harmony Grove P.D. had responded, too. Chief Dalton was there. His car was prominently labeled Chief of Police. If she was lucky, Tommy Patterson was the other officer who'd responded. At least her chances were fifty-fifty.

She swung open the door and before she could step

from the car, a dark-haired, muscular figure crossed the clearing with brisk, sure steps. Alan White. She frowned. Yep, fifty-fifty. She never had been good with odds.

"Hello, Alan." She greeted him with the same stiffness that had characterized their interactions for the past six years.

"Lexi." The stiffness was as pronounced on his end as hers.

She stepped from the car, her gaze shifting upward. A blanket of steel gray wrapped the western sky and a musty-scented breeze whipped the ends of her ponytail into her face. The storm had been building for the past couple of hours, an ever-increasing threat. Now it was more of a promise.

She pursed her lips and swung the door shut. They had their work cut out for them without being hampered by one of central Florida's spring thundershowers. Of course, if this case was like the other four, there wouldn't be anything to gather. The killer had a knack for leaving behind no evidence except a body.

Her eyes circled the area. Up ahead, slashes of yellow interrupted the solid green of the woods. Crime scene tape. She headed in that direction.

Alan fell in beside her. "How much information have you gotten?"

Her gaze settled on him for several moments before she answered. If it was someone they knew, he would have told her up front. "White female, twenty to twenty-five years of age. Punched in the face several times, then strangled."

Same as the others. The pictures hadn't arrived yet. But they would. They always did. The creep got some sick thrill out of photographing his crime, step by step, and sending the pictures to the *Ledger*. Fortunately, the newspaper had turned them over to Lakeland P.D. right from the start, without a single one going to print.

"Is that all you've been told?"

"She was found by a couple of teenagers walking their dog in the woods."

Lexi stopped at a section of the yellow tape stretched between two trees. A few feet away Shane Dalton, Harmony Grove's chief of police, stood with his back to her. In front of him, two Polk County crime scene investigators took photos. Her colleagues. They would be there for the next several hours, scouring every square inch of the area, combing the body for clothing fibers, strands of hair, bits of skin under the fingernails, anything that might bring them one step closer to linking a person to the crime.

When she reached for the tape, her eyes met Alan's again and she hesitated. Something wasn't right with him. It wasn't just the customary stiffness. Deep creases of concern marked the bridge of his nose and anguish had settled in his blue eyes. What wasn't he telling her? "It's someone we know, isn't it?"

"I'm afraid it is."

She ducked under the tape and when she straightened, Alan had stepped in front of her. He was trying to shield her.

It wasn't necessary. She was a professional. And she wouldn't let her personal feelings get in the way of doing her job. Right now, that job entailed performing the best investigation she could to catch this monster and bring him to justice.

Summoning strength she didn't feel, she pushed Alan aside and moved past Shane Dalton. Not more than fifteen feet away lay a body, partially obstructed by a downed limb. Detective Vickers squatted, sitting on one heel to shoot another photo, further blocking her view. She moved slowly closer, longing with all her heart to run the other direction and never look back, while at the same time needing to know.

She took another step. It was definitely a woman, judging by the clothing: baby-blue silk sleepwear.

"Lexi, wait." Alan put a restraining hand on her arm.

She shook him off. Took another step. And another.

A torso appeared. A silk-clad leg. A bare foot extending from the hem of the pajama bottoms, toenails painted hot pink.

Then Detective Vickers straightened and moved aside, offering her an unobstructed view of their newest victim. Her eyes locked onto the scene and her brain shut down. Alan said something, but the words didn't register.

Matted auburn hair flowed over a blanket of dying leaves. Green eyes, one swollen almost shut, stared unseeing at the leafy canopy overhead. Blood had trickled from a cut on one cheek, but had long since dried. The mouth was hidden behind a piece of neatly applied duct tape, and a blackish-red ring circled the creamy white neck.

No.

Lexi shook her head. The ground seemed to tilt beneath her and she took a stumbling step backward to steady herself. A scream of protest clawed its way up her throat, followed by a wave of nausea that almost brought her to her knees.

Alan's words finally penetrated her befuddled brain, several seconds too late.

"Lexi, it's Kayla."

Alan reached for her, his heart twisting in his chest. The confident air she had stepped out of the car with had evaporated like drops of water on a hot tin roof, and her complexion had grown pasty white against the dark forest-green of her uniform. Suddenly, she seemed broken and vulnerable. And much younger than her twenty-seven years.

A sense of protectiveness surged through him, but she backed away from his advance. He didn't expect any different. She would stand alone before she would accept comfort from him.

He should have told her. He should have blurted it out when she'd first climbed from the car. But seeing her drive up had caught him off guard.

Seeing Lexi always caught him off guard.

He had known the Polk County Sheriff's Office would investigate. The body was found outside the city limits of Harmony Grove. But with all the detectives in Polk County, what were the odds that they would send Lexi?

So instead of preparing her for what she would find, he had plied her for information, hoping she'd already known. He'd been a coward. He hadn't wanted to be the one to tell her.

But he hadn't wanted her to find out like this, either.

Now he was kicking himself. Hard. Actually, he hadn't stopped kicking himself since the moment she'd ducked under the crime scene tape. But this wasn't the first time he had kicked himself where Lexi was concerned.

"Lexi, I'm sorry." He stepped toward her again, wishing he could wrap her in a comforting hug. Just like old times. He settled instead for a steadying hand under her elbow. But that gesture wasn't any more welcome than the hug would have been. She jerked away as if touched by something vile, then spun and began walking back the way they had come. The younger of the two detectives started to follow her— Wayne Blanchard, if he remembered the introduction correctly.

Alan held up a hand. "Let me talk to her."

She probably wouldn't want his brand of comfort. But he knew Lexi, and she wouldn't want a colleague to see her break down, either.

A growing rumble followed him into the clearing, and he cast a glance skyward. Heavy black clouds rolled ever closer, the wall of rain already visible in the distance. He dropped his gaze to the retreating figure headed toward the vehicles.

"Lexi, where are you going?" She didn't need to be driving in her state of mind.

"I'm getting some things I need out of my car."

She couldn't be serious. "You're not really thinking of investigating that back there, are you?"

"I'm not *thinking* about it." She pressed a button on her key fob and the trunk popped open. "I'm *doing* it."

"Lexi, you don't have to do this. Let someone else work this one."

She stopped so suddenly he almost bumped into her. When she spun to face him, her eyes blazed. Her anger wasn't aimed at him, but he still had to stifle a grimace.

"This is *my* case." She jabbed an index finger at her chest. "I'm making it my number-one priority to catch this guy."

Stubborn, as always. He opened his mouth to object, then caught movement in his peripheral vision. Detective Vickers had emerged from the woods and was moving toward them.

Lexi cast a glance at Vickers, some thirty feet away, then turned suddenly and grasped both of Alan's upper arms. "Don't say anything." Her voice was a hoarse whisper. "They'll take me off the case."

"Maybe that would be best."

"No." Her eyes flicked to Vickers again and she lowered her voice even more. "This case is important to me. This creep is preying on women."

His jaw tightened. She was right. Kayla wasn't the first. Although the other murders hadn't happened near Harmony Grove, the sheriff's office had disseminated the information to all the agencies.

Lexi continued, her gaze imploring. "You of all people understand what that means to me."

Yes, he did understand. When her best friend was murdered seven years earlier, it had made an impact on her. Enough that she changed her major from business to law enforcement.

"He's taken Kayla now." She dropped her arms to rest a slender hand on his forearm. "Let me bring him to justice. Please, Alan."

She stared up at him with those pleading green eyes, tears pooled at their lower lashes, and all his arguments dissipated, drifting away on the rain-scented breeze. Somehow, being within ten feet of Lexi always turned his will to mush. He had never been able to deny her anything.

Even her freedom.

He released his breath in a heavy sigh. "All right. I'll leave it be. But if you need to talk, I'm here. I cared for Kayla, too."

All he got from her was a brusque nod.

Detective Vickers strode past them and stopped next to the crime scene van. Alan watched him, and then returned his attention to Lexi.

"Is there anything I can do?"

She started to shake her head, then drew her brows together. "Have Aunt Sharon and Uncle George been told yet?"

"I doubt it. No one had an ID until Shane and I arrived right before you did. Would you like me to talk to them?"

Relief flooded her features. "I'd really appreciate it if you would."

He nodded slowly, hesitant to leave her. But she would be all right. She would throw herself into her work and, at least for a brief time, be able to look at the situation through the impartial eyes of a homicide detective.

Then she would drive back to Auburndale, to her empty house. And there would be nothing to distract her. In those quiet, lonely hours, that was when it was the hardest. He knew. He understood. And he would give anything to be there for her.

But she had made her choice. Six years ago. Back then, he'd had hope in his heart, a ring in his pocket and a love that he'd thought would last for eternity. And she'd decided her future would be brighter with an up-and-coming medical-school student than a small-town cop.

Making his way to his patrol car, he slid into the driver's seat and shut the door as the sky opened up and proceeded to dump its burden. Through the rain-drops on the windshield, he watched as Lexi shrugged

"Lexi, you're the spitting image of the target. I'm worried about you."

She tensed. "I know. I saw the photo."

"What if the killer has realized that fact, too?"

"I'm being careful." She put her hands on his cheeks. "If we're going to make this work, you have to accept the risks and trust me to make the right decisions."

"All right." Alan should probably step back and give her space. But he couldn't get his feet to obey.

She brushed a kiss across his lips. "I'll call when I get home. I promise."

He stood frozen, fighting for control. Finally, he stepped away and forced a smile.

"All right. If I don't hear from you within thirty minutes, I'm sending out the search party."

As he watched her back out the drive, his heart stuttered. Somewhere out there was a killer. And Lexi was vulnerable.

After six long years, he was so close to winning her back. He couldn't lose her again.

Books by Carol J. Post

Love Inspired Suspense

Midnight Shadows
Motive for Murder
Out for Justice

CAROL J. POST

From medical secretary to court reporter to property manager to owner of a special events decorating company, Carol's résumé reads like someone who doesn't know what she wants to be when she grows up. But one thing that has remained constant through the years is her love for writing. She started as a child, writing poetry for family and friends, then graduated to articles, which actually made it into some religious and children's publications. Several years ago (more than she's willing to admit), she penned her first novel. In 2010, she decided to get serious about writing fiction for publication and joined Romance Writers of America, Tampa Area Romance Authors and Faith, Hope & Love, RWA's online inspirational chapter. She has placed in numerous writing contests, including RWA's 2012 Golden Heart®.

Carol lives in sunshiny central Florida with her husband (who is her own real-life hero) and writes her stories under the shade of the oaks in her yard. She holds a bachelor's degree in business and professional leadership, which doesn't contribute much to writing fiction but helps a whole lot in the business end of things. Besides writing, she works alongside her music minister husband singing and playing the piano. She also enjoys sailing, hiking, camping—almost anything outdoors. Her two grown daughters and grandson live too far away for her liking, so she now pours all that nurturing into taking care of three fat and sassy cats and one highly spoiled dog.

OUT FOR JUSTICE
CAROL J. POST

HARLEQUIN® LOVE INSPIRED® SUSPENSE

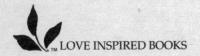 ™ LOVE INSPIRED BOOKS

Recycling programs
for this product may
not exist in your area.

ISBN-13: 978-0-373-67614-9

OUT FOR JUSTICE

www.Harlequin.com

Printed in U.S.A.

Trust in the Lord with all your heart and lean not on your own understanding; in all your ways acknowledge him, and he will make your paths straight.
—*Proverbs* 3:5–6

Thank you to my family for your unending support and encouragement. And thanks to my sister Kim, who helped me plot this story during Christmas vacation.

Thank you to my critique partners,
Karen Fleming, Dixie Taylor and Sabrina Jarema.
You always help me make my stories better.

And thank you to my editor, Rachel Burkot, and my agent, Nalini Akolekar. You're both the best!

Thank you to my husband, Chris.
After 34 years, you still put romance into my life.

into a raincoat and pulled its hood over her head. It was going to be a long night for her.

He had often wondered if she had regrets. Things obviously hadn't turned out as she had hoped because she was still single. But during all of their chance meetings over the past six years, she had never hinted at any interest in reigniting old sparks. She always eyed him with a sort of uneasy coldness, coupled with underlying hurt and anger.

As if *he* was the one who had dumped *her*.

He pulled onto the road, serenaded by the roar of the downpour and the *swish-swish* of the windshield wipers. A knot of dread settled in the pit of his stomach. Kayla was George and Sharon's only child. They wouldn't handle the news well. Neither would the class of second-graders who would return from spring break next week to find their beloved Miss Douglas gone. Kayla's absence would leave a hole in a lot of lives.

When he pulled into the Douglases' driveway, the garage door was up. The white Escort sat on the right, but the spot reserved for George's Silverado was vacant. Which meant Sharon was home alone.

He got out of the car, the knot in his stomach swelling to boulder size. He would stay with Sharon until George arrived. Then maybe he would go have dinner at Pappy's. Not that he would feel like eating. But the hometown pizzeria was always hopping.

In Harmony Grove, news traveled fast. And the more shocking the news, the faster it spread. Maybe

Kayla said something. Or maybe someone saw something. He would look for any shred of evidence that might help them find whoever had done this to her.

Lord, help us catch this guy before anyone else gets hurt.

His thoughts turned to Lexi and a pang of tenderness shot through him. She was probably at that moment working on her investigation, doing her best to hold it together, the rain masking tears she would try so hard not to shed.

And, Lord, please give Lexi the strength to do what she feels she needs to do.

TWO

Lexi straightened her spine and tried not to fidget. A couple dozen other detectives sat at tables around the room, and Tomlinson stood at the front ready to bring everyone up to speed on the latest developments in the case.

The weekend had been a blur and hadn't included nearly enough sleep. By the time she had gotten home and crawled into bed in the wee hours of Saturday morning, it had been almost daylight. But even then, sleep had eluded her. Every time she got just on the brink, the image of Kayla—bound, gagged and strangled—shot through her mind and jolted her instantly awake.

And Saturday and Sunday hadn't offered any opportunities for rest. All the daylight hours and a fair share of the nighttime ones had been occupied with family. Aunt Sharon and Uncle George were a wreck, so Lexi had jumped in with making phone calls, helping with funeral arrangements and securing lodging for those who would be traveling to attend the service.

Now she was beyond exhausted. If she sat in one place for too long, she would probably fall asleep. Hopefully, Tomlinson would keep it short.

When the sergeant stepped up to the podium, his expression was grave. His eyes circled the room. "Thursday night, our killer struck again. The newest victim was Kayla Douglas, a twenty-four-year-old teacher at Harmony Grove Elementary. She was found in the woods Friday afternoon, about three miles north of town."

Tomlinson's gaze shifted to Lexi and lingered. If he was looking for a reaction, he wasn't going to get one. No way was she going to give him a reason to pull her off the case.

Finally he continued, "The photos arrived at the *Ledger* in Saturday's mail. They're being processed now, along with the envelope."

Just like the others. Lexi sighed. It almost seemed a pointless waste of time. The killer had never left behind any prints. No DNA on the envelope seal or the back of the stamp. He used one of the well-known brands of envelope sealers. He was too smart to lick them. Or to touch anything without gloves.

But as long as he kept killing, they would keep investigating each case as if it was the first. Because eventually they would get a break. When someone kills long enough and frequently enough, no matter how meticulous and methodical, he eventually makes a mistake.

Tomlinson moved out from behind the podium

to pace slowly back and forth across the front of the room. "We've checked out her house and lifted some prints from the entry area. But just as with the other women, there was no sign of a struggle, and the neighbors didn't hear a thing. If she disappeared from home, she went willingly. Or at least opened the door willingly. It'll be a while till we get the toxicology report back, but my guess is they'll find chloroform in her system, too."

Lexi struggled against the churning in her gut. How could Kayla have fallen prey? She was smart, always cautious. But according to friends and family members, so were the other victims. These weren't women who hung out in bars and went home with strange men. They were careful, responsible girls who disappeared from their own locked homes after being settled in for the night.

"As most of you know, this is the fifth one. And the killer's M.O. is always the same. He shows up at the homes of his victims, somehow convinces them to open the door, then puts them out with chloroform. And before he leaves with his unconscious victim, he meticulously twists the lock and pulls the door shut behind him."

He stopped his pacing and faced them fully. "We're already working with Lakeland, Winter Haven and Bartow. Now we're going to involve Harmony Grove. So, Simmons, coordinate your efforts with them. I'm guessing you know the chief of police and the two officers."

She nodded. Oh, yes, she knew them. One better than the others.

Six years ago he had offered her a ring. And she had panicked. She was finally ready to claim her independence and, based on her parents' miserable relationship, decided she was better off alone. She'd left for school, hoping deep down that he loved her enough to wait for her. He waited, all right. Maybe a week. She'd come home during Thanksgiving break ready to tell him she had made a mistake. He'd met her at the door…with his new fiancée. *Pregnant* fiancée, if the rumors were to be believed.

Since then, even though her mom still lived in Harmony Grove, she and Alan had pretty well managed to avoid each other. The first two years, she'd been away at school. Then, instead of returning to Harmony Grove, she'd settled in nearby Auburndale. Up until Friday, they had seen little of each other.

Something told her that was about to change.

Tomlinson resumed his pacing. "The Harmony Grove officers likely know everyone in town, so they should be able to help us. I want the names of every person she came in contact with for the past month, and every possible lead followed. There's got to be some connection between these five women, someone they each knew and trusted well enough to open the door for late at night."

"Yes, sir." She wouldn't leave any stone unturned. Even if it meant working side by side with Alan.

Tomlinson returned to the podium and rested both

hands on its top edges. "The story has already hit the papers, and at some point we'll call another press conference. But we have to be careful. There's a fine line between warning the public and giving this guy the fame and recognition he wants."

He inhaled slowly. "A lot of killers like to keep trophies, but this guy is different. He wants his crimes on display for the world to see. Right now he's killing at the rate of once a month. Seeing his actions publicized could spur him to kill more." Tomlinson's gaze circled the room. "All right, then. Let's get out there and get this thing solved."

Lexi dropped her pen into her purse and gathered her notepad. So she was going to have to work with Alan. She could handle it. At least Tomlinson hadn't taken her off the case.

She moved across the room and as she reached the open door Tomlinson's voice stopped her.

"Simmons, hold up. I need to talk to you."

She paused in the doorway, apprehension sifting over her. Maybe she was premature on her assessment that he wasn't going to pull her. "Yes, sir?"

"Are you okay working this case? I heard you almost lost it out there."

Embarrassment surged through her and her stomach clenched. Blanchard or Vickers. One of them had squealed on her.

Either that or Alan had broken his promise and made a call to her supervisor.

"I'm fine, sir." Her gaze traveled past Tomlinson to where a new detective was making his way toward them from the restrooms. Greg something. She had met him once or twice. And she didn't want him knowing her business. Nothing against Greg. He seemed like a nice enough guy. But she didn't want *anybody* knowing her business.

She waited till he passed, then turned her attention back to Tomlinson.

"Sir, Harmony Grove is a small town, and I grew up there. So I knew the victim." That was all she would tell him.

"I suspected as much. I can assign someone else."

"No, sir, that won't be necessary."

He studied her, his kind eyes searching, and she fought the urge to squirm under his gentle scrutiny. Brent Tomlinson was like a father to everyone in the district.

"Is there something you're not telling me?"

She shook her head. "I can handle it, sir."

He hesitated for only a moment longer. "Then get out there."

Relief washed through her. "Yes, sir. I'll do that."

"Maybe with a lot of luck and some really great detective work, we'll catch this guy." He smiled, crinkling the skin at the corners of his eyes. "And a little prayer wouldn't hurt, either."

She nodded. The really great detective work—she was all over that. But the prayer would have to be someone else's department. She and God weren't on speaking terms. Hadn't been for quite some time.

Seven years, to be exact. Not that they had been all that close before.

But when God had taken her best friend, that had cemented it. Of course, even now, she had to admit that God hadn't exactly taken her. Greed and bad choices had gotten Priscilla killed. And blackmailing some really bad dudes.

But it hadn't been that way with her dad. He hadn't done anything to bring about his demise. He'd spent his entire adult life catering to an impossible-to-please woman. Then three years ago, he'd come home from work, sat down with the newspaper and keeled over with a massive heart attack.

And now her cousin Kayla. Kayla was the kindest, most generous person she had ever known. She poured her life into her students, tithed her 10 percent and never missed a church service.

But God had taken her anyway.

No, if that was the kind of God people served, someone else would have to do the praying.

A steel-gray sky hung low over the manicured lawns of Peace Memorial Gardens, and a light mist rained down on those gathered around the freshly dug grave. The weather fit the mood.

Alan had joined the others who had made the short trip from the Cornerstone Community Church to the cemetery at the edge of town. Most of Harmony Grove had come out for the funeral, and the small brick church had been filled to capacity and beyond.

He had arrived ten minutes before the start of the service and had had no choice but to squeeze in along the back wall. Lexi, he had assumed, was seated at the front with the family.

But the group attending the simple graveside service was much smaller—about three dozen of Kayla's closest friends and family members. Pastor Tom stood in front of the casket, in the center of the elongated semicircle of mourners.

Alan cast a glance at Lexi some six feet away. The simple black dress she wore emphasized the paleness of her skin, and crystalline mini-droplets coated her blond hair, giving her an almost ethereal quality.

She stared straight ahead, her shoulders stiff and her jaw rigid. He understood. He felt it, too—anger at whoever had done this to Kayla.

But Lexi's anger was also directed at God. At least it had been before, when her best friend was killed. Back then he hadn't had any answers for her. He hadn't shared any godly wisdom, because he'd had no faith of his own.

Now he did. He had that faith. And he knew where Kayla had gone. But he still didn't have any answers.

After Pastor Tom gave the closing prayer, the small crowd began to disperse. Alan fell in beside Lexi as she walked toward her car.

"Are you doing all right?"

She shrugged. "As well as can be expected."

"Anything I can do?" He had talked to Chief Dalton about the county and city coordinating efforts to find Kayla's killer. The chief had thought it was a great idea and said he would talk to the sheriff's office. Hopefully the sheriff's office agreed. Kayla had been a good friend. He wanted the creep caught. And it would be that much more rewarding if he could have a personal hand in it.

"Actually, there is." She stopped next to her car and turned to face him. "Get in."

He hurried around to the passenger's side of the blue Mazda before she could change her mind. By the time he slipped inside, she was already sitting at the wheel, her gaze fixed on some point beyond the spotted front windshield.

"It looks like we're going to be working together. At least coordinating our efforts." She spoke without looking at him. She didn't sound thrilled. But she didn't seem miffed, either.

"Are you okay with that?"

Now she looked at him. "We both want to see Kayla's killer caught. I think we're mature enough to set aside our past differences and work toward the same end."

He nodded. "The sheriff's office has filled us in on each of the cases. But give me everything you've got."

"The girls were all early to mid-twenties, two from Lakeland, one from Bartow and one from Winter Haven. The perp feeds on recognition, so he takes photos of his victims and sends them to the *Ledger,* hoping they'll be printed."

"Have they been?"

"No. They've turned them over to Lakeland P.D., who has turned them over to us."

"I guess responsible journalism exists after all."

He gave her a wry smile. She might have even returned it. Just a little.

She continued, expression again somber. "Sometimes we get the photo before we find the body. Sometimes we find the body first."

"Kayla?"

"The photos arrived Saturday."

He clenched his fists. It wasn't enough that the creep had to kill her. He'd furthered his thrill by photographing his work. Alan's jaw tightened. Whatever it took, he was going to catch this guy.

"So what can you tell me about these murders?"

"I don't know about Kayla, but with the other four, friends or family members have stated that they knew for a fact that the girls were home for the night and not planning to go back out."

"Kayla, too."

She looked at him sharply. "You're sure?"

"Positive. She was with me that evening. I dropped her off at her house at nine-thirty."

Her eyes raked over him. "You were dating Kayla, too? You get around."

The sarcasm in her tone stabbed at him. "No, it wasn't like that. She needed to buy a gift and conned me into driving her to Lakeland Square Mall."

"Uh-huh."

Her response was heavy with skepticism. So he

dated a lot. Big deal. Single at thirty-two, he had gained the title of Harmony Grove's most eligible bachelor. But that wasn't saying much. There were only a handful of single guys his age.

At least he kept it casual. He wasn't out to break any hearts. His dates were more friendship than anything.

Several years ago he had been ready to commit. To Lexi. She had turned him down flat. In his naïveté, he had held out hope she would come around.

He should have seen the writing on the wall. When she'd insisted she didn't want to tie him down while she did her last two years of school out of state, he had believed her. And even though he'd been willing to wait, when she'd suggested they date other people, he had reluctantly agreed.

It hadn't taken her long to replace him. Not long at all. What really stung was that she hadn't had the guts to tell him herself. She'd sent her mother to do it. The message was that Lexi had found someone else. The implied meaning was that this bright, young medical student was worthy of her, and he somehow wasn't. Her rejection had set him up for a whole series of bad choices of his own.

But this wasn't the time to dwell on past mistakes. They had a murder to solve.

"Is there any link between the victims? Jobs, friends, places they frequent?"

Lexi shook her head. "None that we've been able to find. The first four had no friends in common, didn't hang out at the same places and had totally unrelated careers. One was an administrative assistant and one was a dental hygienist. The other two were students at two different colleges. One went to Florida Southern and the other to Polk State."

"How about physical description? Any particular body type or hair color he's targeting?"

"Nope, they go all the way from a petite one hundred eight pounds to a hefty two-thirty. And we've got a platinum blonde, a dishwater blonde and two brunettes. And now, with Kayla, a redhead."

Lexi heaved a sigh and continued, "The only similarities are their ages and the way they're killed. He chloroforms them, takes them into the woods, and after they wake up, bloodies them up a little, then strangles them." Sadness filled her gaze and she lowered her voice. "We know they're awake because of the pictures."

Alan closed his eyes, a vise squeezing down on his stomach. These weren't nameless girls she was talking about. This was Kayla.

Lexi let her head fall back against the headrest and stared out the windshield. "Our best clue at this point—our *only* clue—is that the killer is someone each of the victims knew well enough to feel comfortable unlocking and opening their door late at night. But it has to be a newer acquaintance, or their friends and family members would be aware of him. And so far we haven't gotten a single match."

Alan thought for a moment. Who could each of

these women have met recently who would be un-known to friends and family members? "What about workers—cable or phone techs, carpet cleaners, plumbers, electricians, anything like that?"

Lexi frowned. "Nothing that matches. One of the Lakeland girls had Stanley Steamer clean her carpets three weeks before she was killed. The one in Winter Haven had cable installed two months before she died. The other two didn't have any kind of work done, at least nothing that shows up on receipts, credit card statements or banking records."

Alan nodded. "So what now?"

"Talk to everyone we know in Harmony Grove who might have any information."

"I've already talked to her neighbors. No one saw or heard anything that night. Well, I take that back. Old Mrs. Thayer saw me pull up, get out and walk Kayla to the door."

She cocked a brow at him. "That just might make you our only suspect. Have you ever met Meagan Bowers, Stephanie Wilson, Donna Jackson or Sylvia Stephens?"

"Nope, never heard of them."

She gave him a quirky grin. "Okay, then you're probably not the killer."

"I hope your interrogations aren't always that easy."

"No, they're not. Usually I'm a tough interrogator." She grew serious again. "Look, keep everything I've told you under wraps. Tomlinson is afraid if we give him the publicity he wants, it'll just encourage him to kill again."

"Will do."

He climbed from the car, then poked his head back inside. "Lexi, be careful. You're in that age group."

"No, I'm not, I'm two years past."

She was right. But with her soft features and girlish smile, she could easily pass for twenty-five. Or younger. "Close enough. So be careful."

"Don't worry, I'm not the type to open my door to anyone in the middle of the night."

"Neither was Kayla."

THREE

Lexi walked down the hall of Harmony Grove Elementary School amid the awed stares of first-and second-graders. Since one school resource officer was assigned to several elementary schools in the area, it wasn't often that the munchkins of Harmony Grove saw a uniformed police officer walking their halls. Especially one who carried a gun.

The release bell had just rung and teachers were herding their unruly charges toward the pickup area. Kayla's classroom was up ahead. Third door on the left. Someone needed to clear out her things. And Aunt Sharon was in no shape to deal with it.

Lexi had another reason for showing up at Kayla's school. She had arranged to meet with a couple of teachers who'd been close to her. Maybe they would remember something she had said before she died, something that had seemed insignificant at the time but could be important in solving the case. So far she and Alan had come up with zilch.

When she stepped into Kayla's classroom, a woman

stood facing the front, wiping a rag across a chalk-board in smooth arcs. Two plastic crates sat atop the wooden desk. Lexi cleared her throat and the woman spun to face her.

"Oh, hi. You must be Lexi. I'm Jenny, the substitute filling in until they get someone permanent." She put the cloth in the chalk tray. "They told me you were going to be coming, so I gathered up Kayla's things." She motioned toward the two crates filled to over-flowing with books and various items.

Lexi picked up a box from the top.

"Cuisenaire rods," Jenny explained. "They're math manipulatives."

Lexi nodded. Beneath that were sets of flash cards and a variety of children's books. She placed the items back into the box. "Are these things you can use with the students?"

"You betcha."

"Then how about if I leave them here?" Better than letting them collect dust in a closet. Aunt Sharon would probably agree.

Lexi emptied the other box, then repacked every-thing a minute later, keeping out three framed pho-tos and several objects that had most likely been gifts from students. Those items Aunt Sharon would trea-sure.

Jenny flashed her an appreciative smile. "Thank you for donating all the educational things. I know the students appreciate it."

"No problem. I'm glad they'll get some use out of them."

She started to walk toward the door, Jenny next to her. "How well did you know Kayla?"

"I'm afraid I didn't. This is my first time subbing at Harmony Grove. But everyone says she was a special lady. Well loved. She's going to be a hard one to follow."

Jenny pulled the door shut behind them and removed a key from her pocket. She was young, probably not more than twenty-three or twenty-four, with clear blue eyes that still held a touch of youthful innocence. And if the lack of a wedding band was any indication, she was probably single. Which meant she was as likely as anyone to be the killer's next victim.

And completely oblivious to the danger.

"Do you live alone?"

Jenny raised her brows in question. "Yes, why?"

"Just be careful. Don't ever open the door to anyone at night without calling the police first."

Jenny nodded slowly. "O-kay."

Lexi waved farewell and headed toward the teacher's lounge, leaving the young substitute to ponder the warning. If Kayla had fallen prey to the killer, no one was safe.

"Lexi." The call rang out just as she reached the open door of the teacher's lounge. She turned to see both Evie and Miranda hurrying toward her.

She smiled at Kayla's two best friends. "Thanks for staying to talk to me." If anyone had little-known information that could help solve the case, it would be these two teachers.

Miranda sank into a chair at one of the four round tables. "You know we're happy to help in any way we can. We want this monster caught as much as anyone."

Evie sat opposite Miranda and Lexi settled in next to her.

"Do you know of anyone who would have wanted to hurt her?"

Evie clasped her hands together on the table and frowned. "Everyone loved Kayla. I don't think she ever made an enemy."

"Had she mentioned being afraid? Anyone following her or taking an unusual interest in her?"

Miranda shook her head. "If there was, she never mentioned it."

"Did she mention meeting anyone new recently?"

"Kayla was always meeting someone new." Evie smiled wryly.

Evie was right. Kayla was outgoing and bubbly, the kind who struck up conversations with cashiers and gas station attendants. She never met a stranger.

"Anyone specific that she mentioned?"

Evie answered immediately. "Not that I know of."

"Wait." Miranda held up a finger. "There was the water guy."

Lexi raised her brows. "Water guy?"

"Oh, yeah." Evie leaned forward in her chair. "How could I forget? Some guy trying to sell her one of those whole house water-filtration systems. He kept checking back. Didn't want to take no for an answer."

Lexi's heart started to pound. Was this the link between all the victims? It was possible. Nothing had turned up, but if they hadn't purchased a system and thrown away the guy's card, there would be no trail. "Did she mention a name, or a company that he was with?"

"I don't think so." Miranda looked at Evie, who shook her head.

Lexi pulled out two of her cards and scribbled her cell number on the backs. "If anything else comes to mind, call me."

As soon as she reached the parking lot, she punched in Alan's number. He answered on the third ring.

"What are you doing?" she asked.

"Getting ready to mow the lawn. Why?"

"So you're off duty."

"I can put myself back on duty. What's up?"

"I'm headed to Kayla's. I've got a lead."

"I'll meet you there in ten minutes."

She dropped her phone into her purse and hurried toward her patrol car, ready to turn her cousin's house upside down if necessary. Kayla wasn't a pack rat, but she wasn't a total neat freak, either. Hopefully she'd left behind some kind of clue. An estimate. A business card. Anything that could help them find this mystery water-filter salesman.

Because it was the only lead they had.

* * *

Lexi moved up the sidewalk that bordered a bed overflowing with day lilies and blooming spring annuals. She closed her eyes and breathed in the scented air. Kayla loved her flowers. Every Saturday, she'd spent two or three hours piddling in the yard, weeding, watering, fertilizing and pruning. And all the tender loving care showed.

But Lexi wasn't there to admire the landscaping. If she was lucky, the break they were hoping for waited somewhere inside the small two-bedroom house.

She took the key she had gotten from Aunt Sharon and pushed it into the lock. The crime scene investigators were finished with their work. Fine black powder still coated the door and jambs. The results hadn't come back yet. Otherwise, they hadn't found anything of note.

But they hadn't been looking for a certain salesman's business card.

She pushed the door open and stepped inside, instantly struck by the cold and empty feel of the house. The place had always seemed warm, cozy and full of life, qualities that had obviously come from Kayla's presence there.

She took in a deep breath and headed toward the spare bedroom. A soft knock on the front door interrupted her midstep. Good. Alan had arrived. The thought of having company filled her with an unexpected sense of relief. Even though that company came in the form of one local cop whom she'd spent the better part of six years trying to avoid.

She swung open the door. Alan stood on her cousin's front porch, clad in jeans and a T-shirt. His yard-work attire. The shirt molded itself to his muscular chest, ending just past the waistband of his snugly fitting jeans. Definitely the body of a sworn protector of the innocent.

But she wasn't going to notice that. She snapped her gaze back to his face and stepped aside. "Come on in."

She worked with buff, athletic cops every day and didn't give them more than a casual glance. Alan was no exception. Whatever they'd had in the past, it had obviously meant more to her than it had to him.

Giving Alan his freedom had initially been her mother's suggestion. It wasn't fair to make him wait for two years while she was away at school. That was the way her mom worked, her control techniques so subtle that her victims hardly realized they had been manipulated. So when Alan had floored her with his marriage proposal, those had been the first words out of her mouth.

By Thanksgiving break, she had realized her mistake and come back to tell Alan. She'd known he was dating. Casually, he had said. Just friends. At his cool greeting, her stomach tightened. When Lauren appeared next to him, her stomach clenched. And when Lauren showed off her sparkly new diamond, her stomach almost emptied its contents. Somehow she'd made it through the congratulations and well wishes without embarrassing herself by losing her lunch or dissolving into a weeping puddle on the porch.

Her mom had gotten her wish. Lexi hadn't married a cop. Instead, she'd become one.

Alan stepped into the house and closed the door. "So what's our lead?"

"A salesman of water-filtration systems." She shook off the last remnants of regret and led him toward the second bedroom, which Kayla had set up as a combination guest room/den. "I talked to Miranda and Evie at the school today. Some guy tried to sell Kayla one of those whole-house water-filtration systems. And according to Miranda and Evie, he was pretty persistent, kept contacting her."

"So what are we looking for?"

"A card, a proposal, a contract—anything that might have this guy's information on it."

Alan picked up the trash can under the desk. It was empty except for one wadded-up piece of paper. A grocery list.

A business-card holder sat near the back of the desk. Lexi removed the cards and thumbed through them. There were about a dozen, mostly from stores around town. None had anything to do with water-filtration systems.

After almost an hour of searching, she heaved a sigh. "I'm guessing she threw it away. We'll go ahead and contact the companies in the area that sell those things and see if any of them had Kayla down as a potential customer."

"I have one more place to check." He headed back into the kitchen and opened the narrow pantry door. A vague odor of garbage hit her nostrils when he took the lid off the trash can. It wasn't very full. Kayla must have taken the trash out the day before she was killed.

Alan tipped the can and poured its contents onto the tiled floor. A plastic grocery bag stuffed with papers sat amid salad and other food scraps. Most of the discarded paper was junk mail. Lexi picked up the sheets and inspected them one by one, then released a sigh.

"Unless there are clues on the backs of these cucumber peels, I'd say we struck out here."

Alan scooped everything up and dropped it back into the can. "I suppose I ought to take this out before it gets really ripe."

She started to put the empty can back into the pantry but a small piece of paper in the bottom caught her eye. Something must have fallen in beside the trash bag. Or was tossed in before the bag was inserted.

She reached into the can and pulled out a business card: Martin Jeffries. All-Pure Water Treatment.

"Bingo."

They finally had a suspect.

Alan opened the door to warehouse number seven in Thompson Commercial Park and let Lexi go in ahead of him. All-Pure Water Treatment was a bare-necessities no-frills kind of place. Fabric-covered office partitions segregated an area on one side of the room and a metal desk stood near the opposite wall. Except for a photo frame on the desk, a clock on the wall and one of those fake ficus trees in the corner, the space was devoid of any decorative touches.

A young woman sat at the desk, a phone propped against her shoulder. Her eyes widened as he and Lexi stepped inside, both in uniform, but she continued her conversation.

Alan pulled the door shut behind them and waited for her to finish. Maybe *conversation* wasn't a good word for it. *Pitch* was more accurate. Apparently, All-Pure had gotten back the results of the free water test, and there were some serious issues with the water. But she, of course, had a specialist she could send to explain the details and present some options. Why drink tainted water when a person could have all the pure water he would ever need for just pennies a day?

The pitch was apparently successful because she jotted a name in the appointment calendar that lay open in front of her, then hung up the phone, smiling.

"How can I help you?"

Lexi stepped forward. It was her case. Things would go more smoothly if he let her lead.

"Do you have a Martin Jeffries who works here?"

Concern flashed across her features. "Is he in some kind of trouble?"

"No, we just need to ask a few questions." Lexi

pulled out a business card and handed it to her. "Do you keep a list of his appointments?"

"We do." Hesitation filled her tone. "I'm not sure what information I'm allowed to share." She cast an uneasy glance at the cubicle on the other side of the room and, as if on cue, a man stepped out.

"Hi, I'm Buddy Jacobs, the owner of All-Pure." He extended his hand, that salesman air even more pronounced than it had been with the girl securing the appointment. "How can I help you?"

After they each accepted the handshake, Lexi continued, "We need a list of Martin Jeffries's appointments going back, say, six months. Is that something you keep?"

"Of course we do. We don't have anything to hide." He nodded toward the girl. "Anne, go ahead and print out his weekly calls going back to the beginning of October. If the boy's up to no good, I want to know about it."

After several clicks of the mouse, pages began to spill into the printer.

Lexi continued, "How long has he worked for All-Pure?"

"Since September. So about seven months. Moved here from out of state."

"Have any of his customers ever complained about him?"

"A couple of times."

"What kind of complaints?"

Buddy laughed. "He's a salesman. Some people

think he comes off a little too…high pressure. But I can't argue with his sales figures. He's good at what he does."

"Where can we find him?"

"He's off today and tomorrow. Won't be back in until Saturday."

Anne removed the small stack of pages from the printer and handed them to Lexi.

"Do you think Martin might be at home?"

"He might be. I'll have Anne get the address for you. It's new, as of about a month ago. I think he's living with a lady friend."

By the time they got back into Lexi's cruiser, she had added an Auburndale address to the pages of customer appointments. She handed Alan the list and began to program the address into the GPS.

"See if you can find any of the victims' names on those lists."

He picked up the file between the seats—Lexi's notes, duplicates of the information she needed quick and easy access to. While she drove, he read through the names Buddy Jacobs had provided. Halfway down the second page, anticipation surged through him. One name matched.

"In early November, he had an appointment with a Stephanie Wilson in Winter Haven."

"She was the third victim, killed about two months ago. What address?"

"Cypress Gardens Road."

Lexi frowned. "The victim lived in the Inwood area."

"Maybe she moved." He continued to search for the other names, scanning the single-spaced pages. This guy saw a lot of people.

Finally he slid the sheets into Lexi's folder. "That's it. Just Stephanie and Kayla. The others aren't here."

Lexi nodded. "If it's the same Stephanie Wilson, that's two out of five. There's definitely enough of a lead to follow up on. He may have even deleted the other three names. I mean, if you were killing your customers, would you leave that kind of a paper trail?"

"You've got a point. If he had access to the computer."

She turned into an upscale neighborhood and moved slowly down the road until she reached the number she sought. If the grand, two-story Colonial at the end of the driveway was any indication, Jeffries's lady friend had some bucks.

Chimes followed the ringing of the bell, then faded to silence. Apparently no one was home.

Lexi turned to head back to the car. "I'll try again this evening."

Alan shook his head as anxiety spiked through him. "Let me do it."

"I live about a mile that way." She pointed over his shoulder. "It doesn't make sense for you to drive over here from Harmony Grove."

"You shouldn't come here alone."

She reached the patrol car and nailed him with a

withering glare over its top. "This is my case. I know we're working together, but I'm the lead detective."

It wasn't going to do any good to take a stubborn stance with her. When it came to stubbornness, Lexi took the prize. She hadn't always been that way. She had been happy and agreeable and perpetually optimistic. But life's knocks had stamped out most of that youthful innocence and left her with a hard edge. And something told him he had unwittingly contributed to it.

"Look, Lexi, you fit the profile of the victims."

"That's a pretty broad profile."

"Still, you fit it. I don't mind the drive. Let me come back with you."

She hesitated for a moment longer then sighed. "All right. Meet me at my house at eight."

Within moments of turning onto Berkley Road, a gold Lexus moved toward them in the opposite lane, slowing as it approached. A male driver sat at the wheel. As near as Alan could tell, he was the only one in the car. Lexi slowed, casting several glances in her rearview mirror.

"He just turned into Somerset. You think that's our Mr. Jeffries?" She was already turning around as she posed the question.

When they pulled into the driveway, the driver of the car was bent at the waist, removing shopping bags from the front passenger seat. He straightened and spun to face them. His eyes widened. A split second later he dropped the bags in the driveway and shot off toward the right side of the house at a full run, disappearing through a wrought iron gate.

Alan jumped from the cruiser and ran toward the break in the wall. Jeffries was guilty of something. If it was murder, they just might end this thing a lot more quickly than he had anticipated.

If they could catch him.

Alan came to a sudden halt, Lexi next to him. The lavishly landscaped backyard offered numerous places to hide. And Jeffries was nowhere to be seen.

He cocked his head to the left. Lexi gave a slight nod and moved across the back of the house with sure, silent steps. She would make a good partner.

But he didn't spare her more than a brief glance. He moved deeper into the yard, hand on his revolver, eyes peeled for the slightest movement. Manicured hedges wrapped curved walks and a figure of some Greek goddess stood framed on three sides by walls of vine-covered lattice. Somewhere nearby, the gurgle of a fountain masked the sound of their steps.

He had almost reached the back boundary of the yard when Lexi's shout caught his attention. Jeffries had climbed a tree in the corner and was shimmying along a lower branch. Lexi wasn't far behind. She hoisted herself up as Jeffries dropped down to disappear behind the wall.

Alan ran along the back perimeter, heart pounding in his chest. Jeffries had had too much of a head start. And Lexi was confronting him alone.

When he dropped to the ground, Jeffries was limping toward the front of the adjoining yard. He had evidently sprained his left ankle, which was giving Lexi a distinct advantage. She was only about fifteen feet behind.

Suddenly, Jeffries skidded to a stop, and so did Lexi. Alan moved cautiously closer. Only then did he hear the low growl. It increased in volume, then erupted into angry barking.

A Doberman sprang toward Jeffries and Lexi, then stopped, the three forming a wary triangle. The dog alternated between barks and growls, razor-sharp teeth glistening in the afternoon sunlight.

Jeffries crept backward, feeling for the side fence. "Good dog," he crooned. But all he managed to do was to attract the Doberman's full attention. The stance grew more threatening, the growls deeper. The dog inched closer, muscles coiled, ready to spring at any moment.

In a sudden burst of panic, Jeffries spun and lunged for the fence. He was half over when those lethal teeth sank into one calf. Alan cringed at Jeffries's agonized shriek. When the dog pulled, Jeffries lost his grip and fell to the ground in a wail of fear-tinged pain.

"Boomer, heel!"

The command rang out with undeniable authority. The dog froze but didn't relax his posture.

"Thank you." Lexi reached behind her to unhook

a set of handcuffs from her belt. "Is it okay to cuff the suspect?"

The homeowner smiled. "Absolutely. Boomer, come."

Boomer obeyed the order, albeit reluctantly, and Lexi stepped forward to restrain Jeffries. He still lay rocking back and forth on the ground, knee pulled up, clutching his lower leg.

Once Lexi had cuffed him and read him his rights, she straightened and looked at Alan. "How about if you keep an eye on him while I bring the car around. I don't think he's going to be climbing any fences anytime soon." She cast a disdainful glance at the man still writhing on the ground. "And I suppose I'd better call an ambulance."

Alan watched her turn away from Jeffries with a coldness in her eyes that shocked him. He was half surprised she didn't kick him first.

Of course, if Jeffries had killed Kayla, he would do it himself.

He dropped his gaze to their suspect. He seemed to be settling down. Maybe he was going into shock. They would get him some medical treatment. Then they would try to interrogate him.

Maybe by then he would be ready to talk.

FOUR

Lexi braked to a stop at the Lakeland Regional Medical Center emergency entrance. Ahead of them, two paramedics lifted a gurney from the back of the ambulance and wheeled it toward the automatic glass doors.

Calling for an ambulance was probably a good idea. By the time the paramedics arrived, Martin Jeffries had grown pasty white and begun to shiver. In his early forties, he wasn't a prime candidate for a heart attack, but one never knew.

She slanted a glance at Alan. "I'm leaving you to make sure our illustrious Mr. Jeffries doesn't take off."

Alan raised his brows. "Where are you going?"

"I'm going to sit out here and see what I can find out about this Stephanie Wilson. If Jeffries decides to start talking before I get back inside, take good notes."

"Aye, aye, Captain." He lifted his hand in a salute and stepped from the car.

As soon as the ambulance pulled away, Lexi circled around and chose a parking space. She opened her laptop and, within a few minutes, found five listings for Stephanie Wilson. None of the addresses matched the one on All-Pure's paperwork.

When she did a search on the address of All-Pure's Stephanie, the property appraiser listed a Lamar Deeson as the owner. The mailing address was different from the site address, so he apparently didn't live there. Stephanie was probably his tenant.

Since she had hit a dead end looking for Stephanie's contact information, she tried Lamar's. Apparently there was only one Lamar Deeson in all of Winter Haven. And the address matched the mailing address on the property appraiser's website.

He answered on the third ring.

"This is Detective Alexis Simmons with the Polk County Sheriff's Office. I'm looking for Stephanie Wilson. I understand she's a tenant of yours?"

"*Used* to be a tenant of mine."

Lexi's pulse picked up. "Used to be? What happened to her?"

"She left. She and her boyfriend broke up, and she moved out. Then he did, too. Stuck me for two months worth of rent."

"When was this? When did she move out?"

"It would have been in January."

January. A month before Stephanie Wilson was found murdered. Now, as for whether it was the same Stephanie Wilson...

"Do you know where she went?"

"I have no idea."

"How about a phone number?"

"I had a cell phone. Hold on." A minute or two later he came back on the line. "I don't know if it's any good. It just has one of those generic messages, and since I was hounding her for the rent, she never bothered to call me back."

Lexi jotted down the number. "One more thing. Do you get a date of birth or social security number on your tenants?"

"No, I don't bother with all that. I'm not some big property manager. This is my only one. I couldn't sell the place, so I decided to rent it."

"How old would you say Stephanie is?"

"Young. Mid-twenties, maybe."

Her pulse beat faster. "Hair color? Height and weight?"

"Light brown or dark blond. Average height and weight."

"Where did she work?"

"I think she worked part-time at a restaurant. But she was a student."

"What school?"

"I don't know that."

Her heart was pounding in earnest now. Everything fit, right down to her size and hair color. But there was only one way to find out. "I'd like to show you a couple of pictures, see if it's the Stephanie you know. Can I meet with you later this evening or tomorrow?"

"I'm headed out of town in about thirty minutes. But I can meet you when I get back next week." He hesitated. "Did something happen to her? I mean, I'm not identifying a dead body, am I?" He forced an uneasy laugh.

"We're not sure. A Stephanie Wilson was found murdered, but we don't know if it's *your* Stephanie Wilson."

"Oh." The single word was heavy with concern. "She stiffed me for the rent, but I sure don't want to see her dead."

Lexi ended the call with a promise to meet after he returned on Wednesday. Then she tried the cell number Deeson had given her, without success. It was no longer a working number.

When she got inside, Alan was standing in the hall next to one of the triage rooms. An easy smile climbed up his cheeks the moment he saw her, creating an unexpected flutter in her stomach, one she promptly tamped down. He used to have that effect on her, but not anymore. All the butterflies died a quick and sure death six years ago.

She returned his smile with a casual one of her own. "How's Jeffries?"

"The doctor's working on his leg now. Our friend Boomer did quite a number on it."

"Yeah, I gathered as much." Especially with the amount of blood that had soaked through his torn pant leg.

"So what did you find out?"

"She's not there anymore, but I talked to her former landlord. Everything matches victim number three. I'm going to have him look at the photos and tell me if it's the same Stephanie."

Alan crossed his arms and leaned back against the wall. "What about the other three victims?"

"Maybe Jeffries knew them some other way. If we take his picture around to their friends and family members, someone might recognize him."

"Good thinking. We could split the list. You take half and I'll take half."

Before she could respond, a doctor stepped from the triage room and addressed Alan. "Okay, Officer, he's all yours. He'll need to have the stitches removed in another week or so, and he'll have to go through a course of antibiotics. After that, he should be fine."

Alan thanked him and walked into the room.

"Looks like you dropped into the wrong yard." He approached the bed that held a disgruntled Martin Jeffries.

Jeffries responded with a deep scowl.

Alan continued, "We just wanted to ask you some questions. Why'd you run?"

"I didn't know what you wanted."

"It doesn't matter what we wanted. Honest, law-abiding citizens don't run from the police."

"Well, you can't arrest me. I didn't do anything wrong."

Lexi stepped forward. "Actually, we can. It's called

attempting to elude a law-enforcement officer. It happens to be a second-degree felony."

He shrugged off her threat, his attitude growing cockier by the minute. "Whatever. I know how the system works. I won't end up doing more than ninety days, if that."

Alan circled around to the other side of the bed, putting Jeffries between them. "We're doing a murder investigation, and you're looking guiltier by the minute."

The cockiness ratcheted back several degrees and fear flashed in Jeffries's dark eyes. He held up his hands and shook his head. "No way, man. I didn't kill anybody."

Lexi nailed him with an accusing stare. "Then why did you run?"

"Because I thought...I thought Tanya accused me of taking her money."

"We haven't talked to Tanya. Maybe we'll do that later."

Jeffries's gaze narrowed and a muscle tightened in his jaw. He was probably kicking himself for even mentioning it. But he had more to worry about than some pilfered cash.

She leaned closer. "Did you try to sell a water-filtration system to a Kayla Douglas in Harmony Grove?"

"Yeah, I did."

"When did you last see her?"

"About two weeks ago." A flash of annoyance

shot across his features. "What's that got to do with anything?"

Alan provided the answer. "A lot, considering she was found murdered a week ago."

Jeffries shook his head. "You can't pin that on me, man."

"How many times have you been to her house?"

Lexi's question hung in the air for several moments. Then Jeffries pinched his mouth shut. "I'm not saying any more without talking to a lawyer."

"Don't worry. You'll get one." She backed away from the hospital bed. "We'll find out what you're up to with or without your assistance."

A nurse rolled a wheelchair into the room. "Well, Mr. Jeffries, it looks like you're free to go."

"Not exactly free," Lexi interrupted. She watched Jeffries struggle into the chair, then stepped behind it to grip the handles. "You get to come with us."

Jeffries didn't respond. She didn't expect him to. He was done talking. But she wasn't finished with him. Not by a long shot. First she would have him fingerprinted. Then she would see if there were any outstanding warrants for him. And hopefully she could come up with a valid reason to keep him.

Maybe he hadn't killed Kayla.

But he was guilty of something.

Lexi turned off the ignition and frowned over at Alan. "I hope this isn't as much of a bust as our other efforts."

He hoped the same. Over the past several days they had shown Jeffries's photo to at least sixty people. And no one could say they had ever seen him. If Martin Jeffries was the killer, he had managed to keep his relationships with his victims secret from even their closest friends and family members.

Now they were sitting in front of Lamar Deeson's house armed with four photos. The last one they probably wouldn't use. They weren't going for shock value. The first three were plenty sufficient for identification.

Alan stepped from the car and followed Lexi to the door. It was late; the sun had set some time ago. The shades at the windows were drawn, but the glow of the porch light welcomed them up the front walk.

A burly man with hair graying at the temples answered the door.

Lexi stepped forward. "Lamar Deeson?"

At his nod, she continued, "Alexis Simmons. And this is Alan White. Thanks for being willing to do this."

She removed the small stack of photos from a manila envelope and handed him the top one. "Can you tell me if this is the Stephanie Wilson you know?"

The woman in the photo lay on her right side, a bed of decaying leaves beneath her. Her arms were bound behind her and a piece of duct tape covered her mouth. Tangled dishwater-blond hair flowed over her shoulder.

"I—I'm not sure. Looking at her from the side like this, I can't tell."

Lexi handed him another photo. In that one, she sat upright, the trunk of a pine tree supporting her. An angry red splotch marked one cheek, the remnants of an open-handed blow. Above the tape, fear-filled eyes pleaded for mercy.

Deeson shook his head and turned away, mouth set in a grim line. "No, that's definitely not her."

Lexi took the photo from him. "You're sure?"

"Positive." He shook his head again. "I'm sorry. I have a daughter that age. She even looks a little like the girl in the picture." He met their eyes, his own earnest. "I hope you catch the guy who did this."

Alan nodded. "Believe me, we're trying our hardest." He wished he could promise him more.

He walked with Lexi to the car, glad to be heading home. It was draining, talking to person after person. Or maybe it was the fact that they just didn't seem to be getting anywhere. At any rate, it was different from his usual activities: patrolling Harmony Grove, taking old George Randall home when he had had a little too much to drink, getting the occasional kitten out of a tree.

Lexi had just cranked the car when her cell phone rang. After a quick glance at the screen, she put the phone to her ear. Almost immediately she stiffened with anticipation.

"Hold on, Sarge. I'm putting you on speakerphone....Yeah, I'm with Alan. It'll save me having to repeat this."

She plugged in the phone and a male voice came through the car's speaker system.

"As I was saying, the prints came back. Martin Jeffries is an alias. He's actually got several of them. His real name is Victor Moore."

Lexi pulled away from the curb. "So what can you tell us about good ol' Vick?"

"He's not a very nice guy. But he doesn't appear to be a killer. More of a con artist. He gets with women who have money and before they even know what hit them, he's got their bank accounts drained dry and has changed his name and headed off for greener pastures. He's got several warrants out on him for forgery and fraud."

"What about the woman he's been living with?"

"We talked to her, and she did some checking. He's forged a couple of her checks, but hasn't had a chance yet to do too much damage."

Lexi's grip on the wheel tightened. "Good. I'm glad we caught him. Now we know why he ran when he saw us. He figured his latest escapades had come to light. We were lucky on that one."

"Yeah, so was his latest victim. So what have you two learned?"

"We just left Deeson's house, and his former renter is a different Stephanie Wilson. And no one we've talked to has ever seen Jeffries. The only link he has to any of the victims is that he tried to sell Kayla a water-filtration system. So we're back to square one. Five dead girls and not a single lead."

Alan watched her disconnect the call, then ease to a stop at a traffic light. She heaved a sigh, her shoulders sagging.

"After five months of searching for this guy, I thought we had him."

The disappointment in her voice sent a pang of tenderness shooting through him. He rested a hand on her shoulder. "We'll catch him. Eventually we'll get a break. He'll get careless and make a mistake, and we'll nab him."

She turned tired eyes on him. "And how many girls will die in the meantime?"

He dropped his hand. She was right. They had exhausted the only lead they'd had. No mistakes were likely to happen unless he struck again. Their "break" would mean another young woman lost her life.

When she pulled into her driveway twenty minutes later, she turned off the ignition but didn't immediately get out. Since he was in no hurry to leave her, he didn't, either. His Mustang sat next to them, where he had left it early that morning.

She flashed him an appreciative smile. "Thanks for your help today."

"No problem. I want this guy caught as badly as you do."

She sat in silence for a long moment. Then her mouth turned upward in a weak smile. "I don't know about you, but that fast-food burger I had two hours ago really didn't do the trick."

He returned her smile. "Yeah, same here."

"I've got some nachos and killer bean dip if you'd like to come in for a snack."

"Killer bean dip, huh?"

Lexi flinched. "Bad choice of words."

He followed her to the door, where a rocking chair and a potted plant waited on the small front porch. Lexi lived in one of the older Auburndale neighborhoods, with moderate houses, well-kept yards and an obvious lack of bicycles and toys at a good number of them. It was likely one of those neighborhoods where people had put down deep roots, raising their kids then remaining in their empty nests. It held a sense of calm security. Under normal circumstances, he would find that comforting.

But a killer on the loose targeting young women wasn't normal circumstances.

The moment Lexi put the key into the lock, yowling commenced inside. She grinned up at him. "That would be Suki. She's not happy that dinner's late, and she's letting me know."

She twisted the key and opened the door. Just inside sat the source of all the racket—a sleek, slender, blue-eyed cat, mouth open in that low, eerie cry that only Siamese make. Lexi bent to pick her up, and the yowls turned to purrs.

She headed through an open doorway into the kitchen. "I know I promised you nachos and bean dip, but Suki gets fed first. Otherwise she'll drive us crazy."

As soon as she put Suki down, a black cat appeared in the doorway, sized Alan up with big gold eyes, then apparently decided he was okay.

"You have two?"

Lexi gave him a sheepish smile before bending to pick up porcelain dishes with painted paw prints in the bottoms. "Actually, three. After Suki showed up, I decided she needed company, so I adopted Midnight from the Humane Society. Then, two weeks later, Itsy appeared on my doorstep."

As if on cue, a third cat waddled into the kitchen. Alan eyed Lexi doubtfully. "This is Itsy?"

Lexi grinned. "Well, she *used* to be tiny. She's sort of gotten fat."

Alan laughed. Lexi had always had a soft spot for animals. With the toughness she had developed over the past six years, he was glad that soft spot was still there.

He settled into a chair at the small kitchen table while Lexi pulled a Pyrex dish from the fridge. On the other side of the room, all three cats sat in a row, smacking happily.

He eyed the dish in the center of the table. "That looks good."

"It's a seven-layer dip. Although I think this one's actually eight." She put down two plates, dumped a bag of tortilla chips into a bowl and slid into the chair opposite him.

Sitting across the table from her in the warm, cozy kitchen, a sudden sense of intimacy wrapped around him. This was the way it was supposed to have turned out, a lifetime of sharing meals and dreaming dreams. Why had she thrown it all away? Maybe someday he would ask her. Just not tonight.

But whatever her reasons, he'd given up too quickly, then turned to Lauren on the rebound. Of course, she'd made it easy. The instant she found out Lexi had dumped him, Lauren was in hot pursuit. Several years earlier, long before Lexi, it would have been a dream come true. He'd had a crush on her all through high school, a crush he'd kept secret. Prom queens didn't date science nerds.

But for Lauren, things had changed. He was no longer the nerdy geek and she'd found herself in trouble—pregnant and recently dumped herself. Their relationship had been doomed from the start. Lauren had just been using him, and he'd still loved Lexi.

His eyes met hers across the table. "I'm sorry for the way things turned out. I—"

Lexi held up a hand to stop him. "It's in the past. Let's just leave it there."

He nodded and scooped a glob of dip onto a chip. He had wanted to be involved in trying to find Kayla's killer. But maybe working with Lexi wasn't such a good idea.

He cleared his throat. "So where do we go next?"

"Except for a small handful of people we haven't shown Jeffries's photo to, we're done. I'd even be

Out for Justice

willing to be bait. But we have no idea what draws this creep."

A sense of protectiveness surged through him at her words and he tried to tamp it down. She was a trained law-enforcement officer. She was cautious and smart and armed.

And she was alone with her three cats. He'd feel better if Suki was a Rottweiler.

Before he had a chance to tell her so, her cell phone rang. She rose to retrieve it from where she had left her purse on the counter, then cast a glance back at him. "It's Tomlinson again."

Within moments her eyes widened. "We'll be right there."

She disconnected the call and dropped the phone into her purse.

"We just got our big break."

Her eyes shone with excitement and she shifted her weight from foot to foot, unable to stand still.

"Victim number six got away."

FIVE

Lexi lifted the curtain aside and stepped into the sectioned-off area, trying to ignore the ever-present scent of disinfectant. It was her second trip to the emergency room in less than a week, this time Heart of Florida. And she didn't even like hospitals.

The occupant of the bed lay with her head turned, facing the opposite wall where a male figure waited in a chair. Matted brown curls flowed over the pillow, still holding a trapped dead leaf. The shape beneath the thin sheet looked tiny and frail.

Alan followed Lexi into the room, pulling back the curtain in its metal track. The patient slowly pivoted her head. Her lips were broken and misshapen, and one eye was swollen almost shut. A pinkish ring circled her neck, the beginnings of ligature marks. She was lucky. She was alive, and the obvious damage would heal in a short time. Unfortunately, the invisible scars would stay with her the rest of her life.

The moment her gaze fell on Alan, she let out a

startled shriek and scooted away, sheet pulled up to her chin.

The visitor stood and circled the bed, his stance protective. "Get him out of here."

Lexi glanced from the man to Alan, confusion rendering her speechless. But Alan didn't have to be told twice. He was already ducking from the room before she could gather her thoughts.

"I'm sorry." The man moved back to the other side of the bed so he could take the girl's hand. "It was a cop who did this to her."

Lexi's confusion morphed to shock as her stomach did a sudden free fall. Their killer was a cop? "What?"

"At least, he was in an officer's uniform."

So he was a cop or someone impersonating a cop. One small piece of the puzzle fell into place. He didn't know the victims. They opened their doors because they trusted the uniform.

She approached the bed, her mind still reeling. "You're her father, I assume?" At his nod, she continued, "I need to ask her some questions."

She bent to touch the girl lightly on the shoulder. According to the report Tomlinson had, she was twenty-one, but her small form and the fear in her gaze made her appear much younger. "I need you to tell me what happened. Can you do that?"

The girl's eyes filled with tears and she shook her head. Lexi understood. But she had information that could help them solve the case. She was the only one to fall into the clutches of the killer and live to tell about it.

"Honey, I know it's hard." She squatted next to the bed, putting her at eye level with the terrified girl. Her tone was low and soothing. "Right now you just want to forget about everything you went through tonight. But the killer is still out there, and he's going to strike again. We need you to help us stop him. Will you do that?"

After a prolonged silence, she nodded.

Lexi took a notepad and pen from her pocket. "Let's start with your name and where you live."

"Denise Andrews." She gave a Haines City address, her voice paper-thin.

"And you were at home?"

"No."

Lexi's brows shot up. Their meticulous, methodical killer had deviated? "Where were you?"

"Coming home from a friend's house in Kissimmee."

"So what happened?"

"My car broke down and I was on that stretch of 17-92 where there's no cell service. I locked my doors and waited, because I knew if I wasn't home in an hour, my dad would come looking for me."

Mr. Andrews nodded. "She always calls me when she's heading home. She's a good girl. She didn't deserve this."

"No, sir." None of them did. "What happened next?"

"After I had waited about ten minutes, a car drove

past really slow, coming toward me. I looked in my rearview mirror and saw him turn around, come back and park behind me."

"Was it a police car?"

"No. I couldn't tell at the time, because it was dark. But no, it wasn't a police car."

So it probably wasn't a cop. Unless it was an undercover one. "Then what happened?"

"A guy got out of the car and came to my window. He was in uniform. When I saw it was a cop, I opened my door to talk to him. I asked if he could call my dad and let him know I had broken down. He told me not to bother my dad, that he would take me home. He even offered to call someone to have my car towed."

"So what did you do?"

"I got out and went back to his car."

"Can you describe it?"

"It was a light color, like silver or white. I couldn't tell for sure, because it was really dark outside."

"Any idea what kind?"

"I'm not good with cars. It was a four-door. It didn't look new, but it wasn't an old clunker, either."

"You didn't happen to notice any part of the tag number, did you?"

"No, I never went to the back of the car."

"That's all right. So tell me what happened next."

"I got into the front passenger's seat. There was one of those rounded gumball light things sitting on the dashboard."

Lexi nodded. Yep, definitely an impersonator. They

had done away with those gumball lights years ago. All the vehicles now had the lights built in. "Did he get in the car then?"

"No, he said he had to get something out of the trunk."

"Then what happened?"

"I was just sitting there waiting. All of a sudden he opened the passenger door and held something over my face."

"What?"

"A cloth. It smelled sweet, and it made me light-headed and sick to my stomach. I fought to get away, but he was too strong."

While Lexi listened, misty images played across her imagination. But the face she kept seeing was Kayla's.

"What's the next thing you remember?"

"I woke up in the woods. My hands were tied behind my back and he had taped my mouth." A shudder shook her body and she closed her eyes.

Lexi squeezed her arm. "You're doing great, sweetie. What else can you tell me?"

"He hit me and took my picture."

"Did he say anything while he was doing this?"

"He kept calling me Jeanie. He said after ten long years, justice was finally being done."

Lexi scribbled some notes in her pad. The killings were retribution for some perceived wrong. Someone else's wrong. "Did he say anything else?"

"Just that it wasn't supposed to be my time yet,

but how could he resist when I had fallen right in his path."

"What happened then?"

"He hit me again and took two more pictures. Then he put like a rubber strap or something around my neck and started to squeeze." She raised shaking fingers to her throat. "That's when the dog came."

"The dog?"

"I think it was a German shepherd. It came running through the woods, and when the cop guy heard it coming, he hid."

"What happened then?"

"The dog came up to me and started barking. I could hear his owner yelling at him to get back home, but the dog wouldn't listen. Finally the owner found us. He had a flashlight. He untied me and walked me back to his house and called 9-1-1."

Saved by a German shepherd. Denise was one lucky girl.

"Can you describe him—the cop guy?"

"Not really. It was dark."

"Anything at all?"

She closed her eyes, trying to call up a memory she would probably rather forget. "When he went to the trunk, he left the driver's side door open, so the dome light was on. He opened my door, and when he leaned inside, I could see his face. His hair was real short, like a buzz cut, maybe brown, and he didn't have a beard or mustache. His arms were muscular, but I don't know how tall he was, because I never stood close to him."

"Age?"

"Maybe thirties? I don't know."

"Anything else you can tell me that might help us catch this guy? What about the uniform?"

"It was dark, like dark blue or dark green. He had a badge on his pocket and some kind of patch on his sleeve. It looked so real." Her brows pulled together in concentration. "But he wasn't wearing it in the woods."

"What?"

"He had changed. I think he had on jeans and a T-shirt."

Lexi nodded. He probably hadn't wanted to dirty his needed prop. "Anything else?"

Denise shook her head, and Lexi straightened and pulled a business card from her pocket.

"If you remember anything else, give me a call, even if it seems unimportant. A lot of times it's the seemingly insignificant details that help us solve the crimes."

When Lexi stepped around the curtain, she almost bumped into Alan. She dropped her voice to a whisper. "Eavesdropping, are we?"

Alan grinned. "Nope, taking notes. And saving you from having to repeat all that in there."

She walked with him toward the emergency-area entrance. "Now we know why Kayla and the other girls opened their doors."

"And we know this is all about something that happened ten years ago."

The automatic doors slid open and they stepped out into the balmy night air. At almost midnight, only a dozen cars dotted the emergency area parking lot, two of them hers and Alan's. She stopped next to the driver's door of her cruiser.

"The killer is evidently following a particular order in choosing his victims. He's been so methodical and planned everything out so well that he hasn't left behind a shred of evidence. Tonight he deviated. I'm hoping he's going to live to regret it."

She leaned back against the car and crossed her arms. "Tomlinson's getting Crime Scene out there first thing in the morning. But he sent deputies tonight to secure everything so the killer can't go back and cover up any evidence. Of course, there's the span of time between when the neighbor found her and got her back to his house to call 9-1-1."

"Well, I'm praying he overlooked something. Since this one was spur-of-the-moment and not well thought out, there's always that chance."

She nodded absently, her mind stuck on his choice of words. *Praying?* What was it with him and Tomlinson? But she would take whatever help she could get. Because as much as they had learned tonight, they still didn't know what the killer looked like, what he drove or anything about him. Unless there was something really incriminating left behind in the woods, they may as well be looking for a needle in a haystack.

"Do you want me to follow you home?"

She looked up at him with a quirky grin. "Davenport to Harmony Grove, by way of Auburndale? That's a little out of the way, don't you think?"

He grinned back at her. "Maybe a little. But I don't mind. I'm worried about you."

His smile faded and warmth filled his eyes. In the dim glow of the parking lot lights, they had deepened to an almost midnight-blue. He moved closer to rest a hand against her car. If he lifted the other one, he would have her hemmed in. And suddenly that didn't seem like such a bad place to be.

How different their lives would have been if he had waited for her. Would they still be together? What would their chances be if they gave it another shot? She dismissed the thought as soon as it entered her mind. Alan wasn't the "settling down" type. And neither was she.

She stepped aside while she still could and opened the driver's door. "We both need to go home and get some sleep. I'll be fine. I've got my weapon."

She slid into the seat and watched him walk away, a hollow emptiness filling her chest. She tamped it down and took in a cleansing breath. They had a killer to catch. She had no business thinking about captivating blue eyes.

Or second chances.

* * *

Alan cruised slowly down Park Avenue, window down and strains of Third Day streaming through the radio speakers. At eleven o'clock on a Thursday morning, there wasn't a whole lot of police work to do. But after more than a week of making himself scarce, it was time to take up some slack. Chief Dalton had pretty well given him free rein to work on Kayla's case but Tommy, the other Harmony Grove officer, needed some time off.

So here he was, driving through quiet streets, past the sleepy neighborhoods of Harmony Grove, his greatest accomplishment of the morning helping old Mrs. English bring in her groceries. But that was all right. He loved Harmony Grove, and he loved his job.

He put his arm out the window to wave at Delores Griffin, who was halfway through Molly the schnauzer's late-morning walk. The dog had stopped to sniff the base of some shrub that was covered in little blue flowers. Alan took in a breath himself, savoring the scents of spring. It was his favorite time of year. A time of new beginnings and a welcome reprieve before the onslaught of summer's brutal heat and humidity.

As he drove past Pleasant Drive, his gaze traveled down the street. Patty Simmons still lived there, fifth house on the right. The same ranch-style home where Lexi had grown up. Even though six years had passed since he'd made regular trips down Pleasant Drive, it still caught his gaze every time he passed.

If he wasn't careful, his thoughts followed. That was never a good thing. It only led to what-ifs. And mental kicks in the rear.

But keeping the memories at bay was difficult when he was spending almost every day with Lexi. Last night had been the hardest. Maybe it was fatigue. Maybe he was just mentally drained. It had been a long day and heading into the next by the time he'd walked her to her car in the emergency area parking lot.

But seeing her standing there in the glow of the parking lot lights, and thinking about her driving back to Auburndale to her empty house, made him want to wrap her in a protective hug and never let her go.

Fortunately, he hadn't acted on his impulses. Because whatever he was feeling, it likely wasn't returned. Actually, he had no idea if it was or wasn't. But it didn't matter. He didn't measure up. And Lexi wasn't one to repeat her mother's mistakes. Patty Simmons had grown up privileged, her wealthy parents giving her anything she desired. She'd married beneath her, then never got over the fact that her blue-collar husband couldn't keep her in the style she felt she deserved.

Alan pressed the brake as he neared Main Street and turned on his left signal. Booming bass reached him first, reverberating in his chest. The scream of peeling rubber followed. An ancient Impala skidded off Main onto Park, its two inner wheels almost leaving the pavement. A familiar face looked back at him over the wheel, wearing a can't-touch-this smirk.

Great. The Harmony Grove Hellion. Why wasn't he in school? Alan was getting ready to find out.

He brought the siren to life, turned the vehicle around and made his own peel-out turn. Thirty seconds later the Impala eased to a stop on the side of the road.

Alan stepped from the car and approached. The window cranked down in front of the grinning face of Duncan Alcott.

"Why aren't you in school?"

"Because I was bored. I can get Cs and Ds without being there every day."

"Think what you could get if you applied yourself. Do your parents know you're not in school?"

"They don't care."

Unfortunately, the kid was right. With an alcoholic father and a mother who struggled to keep food on the table, sixteen-year-old Duncan's whereabouts were usually an afterthought.

Alan pulled a long rectangular pad from his back pocket and started to write. Duncan's cocky attitude fell away like peeling paint under a sandblaster.

"Hey, man. I wasn't speeding, and there's not a stop sign there, so you can't give me a ticket."

"I'd say taking a ninety-degree turn on two wheels at thirty miles an hour is reckless driving. What do you think?"

He leaned down to look into the car, where Johnny

Davidson sat with wide eyes. At fourteen years old, he had no business hanging with the likes of Duncan.

Alan rested an elbow in the window opening and continued, "And then there's the whole contributing-to-the-delinquency-of-a-minor thing. That one comes with jail time." Of course, Duncan was a minor himself, so the threat was baseless. But Duncan didn't know that.

The kid's eyes widened. "No way. Look, I'll get him back to school right away."

"No, I'd better take him up to Davidson Hardware. Then it'll be up to Mr. Davidson to decide whether he'll want to press charges."

Alan stifled a grin. If there was a contest for who looked more scared, he would have been hard-pressed to choose a winner. Johnny began to shake his head vigorously. "Officer Alan, please don't. My dad will kill me."

"If I let you go, how do I know you won't be right back out here tomorrow?"

"I promise I won't. I'll never skip school again."

"That would be good. Otherwise I'd have to arrest Duncan here. And we don't want that to happen, do we?"

The no came in chorus.

"All right, then. Get back to school." He turned his attention back to his pad.

"You're not still gonna give me a ticket, are you?"

Alan answered without looking up. "Yep."

"Aw, man."

The kid needed to learn a lesson. Granted, he had it bad at home. But he had choices. Hopefully, with consequences, he would start making the right ones.

He watched the Impala turn around and drive away. It would be headed back to Harmony Grove Middle School, no doubt, to return Johnny to his studies. After the car rounded the corner and disappeared, Alan got back into his own car, dropping the ticket pad into the seat next to him.

The ticket pad.

His eyes widened as an almost forgotten memory flashed through his mind. Kayla. A traffic stop. An unmarked car.

Three or four weeks before Kayla had been killed, she'd told him about getting stopped. The car was unmarked, but the officer was in uniform. He'd claimed he stopped her because she hadn't signaled. She'd insisted that she had. He'd run her license, given it back to her and let her go.

Or had he just pretended to run her license?

Had she instead been stopped by a killer in a policeman's uniform driving a car with a gumball on the dash? Maybe he'd taken her license for the sole purpose of finding out where she lived. Is that what he did with all the victims?

He closed his eyes, struggling to call up the conversation. Finally he sighed. If Kayla had given him any details about the car or a description of the person who had stopped her, those facts were buried somewhere deep in his subconscious.

He started up the car and headed toward the station. He had some phone calls to make. If Kayla's license had really been run, there would be a record of it. If not, maybe he had just recalled some valuable information about the killer.

Information they could use to set a trap.

SIX

Lexi lay stretched out on the couch, a half-read paperback in her hands and Suki wedged between her legs. Itsy lay curled up on the floor next to her. Midnight was probably somewhere in the house looking for trouble. The youngest of the three, he had far too much energy and a mischievous streak three miles wide.

She laid the book across her stomach and glanced at the clock: 8:00 p.m. Alan was probably home, winding down for the evening and getting ready for the following day.

Or not. Spending so much time with her was probably putting a major crimp in his social life. Now that he had a free evening, he wasn't likely to let it go to waste. He was probably out with one of the hopeful single ladies of Harmony Grove. That thought didn't bother her. Really, it didn't.

She once again picked up the book. Whatever Alan was doing, he probably wasn't stretched out, surrounded by cats. Of course, she didn't know that.

He might have a menagerie by now. She hadn't been to his place since the night Lauren had met her at the door with her shiny new engagement ring.

A faint buzz sounded behind her, her phone still on vibrate from a meeting she had attended earlier in the day. She twisted to retrieve it from the end table, and when she glanced at the screen, her heart seemed to beat a little faster. Apparently Alan *wasn't* with one of the Harmony Grove ladies.

"Hey, what's up?" She was smiling, and it came through in her tone.

"I saw Sheriff Judd on the six o'clock news."

"Yeah, it's aired a couple of times." She'd seen it, too. Now that they finally had some information on the killer, everyone had decided it was time for another press conference.

"He definitely got the point across. If I was a young woman, I'd think twice about opening *my* door."

"Same here." Until talking to Denise, they'd really had nothing to report. Now they did. And maybe the information would save a young girl's life. "I'm glad it's out there."

"Yeah, me, too." He heaved a sigh. When he spoke again, it was with uncharacteristic somberness. "I'm worried about you, Lexi. You need to be extracare-ful."

The concern in his voice warmed her from the inside out. After marriage to Lauren, a subsequent divorce and six years of living separate lives, whatever tenderness he had felt for her should be gone.

But it wasn't. If she looked too deeply into his eyes, she saw it—traces of everything he had at one time professed to feel.

Like last night, in the hospital parking lot. He had looked at her with such warmth and tenderness, it had threatened to topple every wall she'd ever erected. If he had tried to kiss her then, she would have probably let him.

"Thanks, but I'll be fine, really."

A distinct beep overrode Alan's reply. She pulled the phone away from her ear and frowned at the display. "Tomlinson's calling. I'll call you back."

She touched the screen to switch calls. At her greeting, Tomlinson's bass voice came through the phone.

"Is this a good time for you to talk?"

"I'm home alone with my cats. What's up?"

"Apparently someone doesn't appreciate all the time and effort you're putting into this."

The ominous tone sent a chill trickling over her. She shook it off. "Of course not. He's scared. He left a live witness."

"He also left a message. For you."

"Me?" Her heart started to pound and her palms grew suddenly clammy. "What kind of message?"

"Sweet and to the point. A single sheet of paper, folded in thirds, taped to a light pole in the sheriff's department parking lot. It had *Detective Simmons* typed across it in about a forty-eight-point font."

She gripped the phone more tightly. The chill

seemed to have headed straight for her stomach, condensing into a solid, icy lump. "What did it say?"

"'Back off. Or you'll be next.'"

Lexi closed her eyes and sucked in a calming breath. "He's grasping at straws. He knows he messed up, abducting Denise without thoroughly planning things out in his usual OCD way. Now there's someone out there who can identify him. And that's got to scare him to death."

"Which is why we've been keeping such a close watch on her."

"She wants to go stay with her aunt and uncle in Ocala. They have a horse farm up there." Lexi had talked to her that morning. Denise wasn't adjusting well. She refused to leave the house and, according to her father, jumped at the slightest sound. A change of scenery would do her good.

"It might be the safest place for her. We'll keep it quiet but alert the authorities up there anyway, just in case. And we'll keep the detectives watching the Andrewses' house even after she leaves."

"Good." Denise's purse had never been recovered. The killer had probably disposed of it in a Dumpster somewhere after he'd looked up her address. His best shot at undoing his mistake would be to finish what he started. If he tried, they would be ready.

Tomlinson sighed. "Just be careful."

She smiled at the words that so closely echoed Alan's of a few minutes ago. "I will."

After ending the call, she redialed Alan.

"So what did Tomlinson want?"

She pulled her lower lip between her teeth and tried not to grimace. Alan wasn't going to be happy. But there was no getting around telling him. That had been Tomlinson's sole reason for calling.

"Someone left me a note."

A heavy silence stretched through the phone. "Who? What kind of note?"

"Short. 'Back off. Or you'll be next.'"

"The killer."

"Or a prankster impersonating the killer."

"Lexi, this isn't good." His tone was thick with worry. "You're a target."

"No, he has my name. That's all. It wouldn't be that hard to get. Polk County isn't L.A. or New York City. We have a grand total of ten homicide detectives. And my name's out there. I think you and I have talked to half the population of the county."

She shifted her position to swing her feet to the floor, disturbing Suki in the process. The cat turned with a scolding meow. "Besides," she continued, "being a target wouldn't be such a bad thing. If he comes after me, I'll be ready for him. I'm quite willing to be bait if it will get me closer to catching Kayla's killer."

"You might be willing, but I'm not."

Something in his tone rubbed her the wrong way. It wasn't his decision. It was hers. "Then I guess it's a good thing for the case that it's not up to you."

"You're making this too personal, Lexi. And I'm

sure Sergeant Tomlinson would agree. This might be a good time to step down."

Her anger flared. She recognized his not-so-subtle attempt at control. She had had plenty of practice. Her mom was the queen of manipulation.

"Don't you threaten me with Tomlinson. I haven't had quite the years in law enforcement that you have, but I'm certainly no rookie. I know what I'm doing."

He huffed out an exasperated breath. "When did you get so stubborn?"

"When did you turn into such a control freak?"

"I'm not trying to control you." His tone was low, but the words were thick with tension. "I'm trying to keep you alive."

"Well, that's not your responsibility." Maybe at one time. But he'd given that up when he'd jumped into bed with Lauren instead of waiting for her. "Look, I'm determined to catch this guy. And I won't be deterred by idle threats—yours or the killer's."

She ended the call and put the phone on the end table with a little more force than necessary.

Alan didn't understand. He would never understand.

She put her all into every case. She had no choice. It was at her very core, a driving need to bring to justice those who held no regard for human life. If her best chance of catching the killer would be to let the department use her as bait, then so be it.

For Kayla, she would do it.

Actually, she would do it for any one of the other four victims, too.

Alan punched in Lexi's number and waited through the first ring. He hadn't spoken with her since last night, when she'd hung up on him. At the moment he probably wasn't her favorite person.

Another ring.

He understood where she was coming from. He wanted Kayla's killer caught, too. But Lexi was too stubborn for her own good.

A third ring.

Maybe she was debating whether to take his call. She was going to have to talk to him sooner or later. But she could always let him stew awhile. If she would pick up the phone, she would agree he had a good reason for calling. He had information on Kayla's case. He had made some phone calls, and it was just as he expected.

Lexi answered midway through the fourth ring.

"Hey. I was afraid you were going to avoid me."

"I thought about it, but I figured you'd just keep calling."

Her tone was flat. Either she seriously didn't want to talk to him or she was joking. He couldn't tell which. He used to know her inside out. But things had changed.

"Look, I'm sorry about last night." An apology never hurt.

"Yeah, me, too."

"I didn't mean to upset you."

"It's all right. I might have gotten a little bit defensive."

A tension he didn't even realize he had seemed to drain from him. Now that they had fallen into a sort of cautious friendship, he didn't like being at odds with her. "Where are you?"

"Leaving Harmony Grove. I checked in on Mom."

"How about swinging by the house? Or better yet, meet me at Pappy's for an early supper. I've got some information on Kayla."

"Can't you just tell me over the phone? I need to get home and feed the cats."

"It's early. If they eat at seven instead of five-thirty, I don't think it'll hurt them. From what I've seen, none of them look to be on the brink of starvation."

"I'm tired."

He picked up his car keys and headed for the door. She was weakening. He could tell.

"Then you could use a relaxing dinner out."

A heavy sigh came through the phone. "All right. But I don't want to stay too long."

"We'll be in and out before the late crowd gets there. I promise."

When he pulled into Pappy's parking lot, the blue Mazda was already there.

Edith DelRoss led him to a booth in the back, where Lexi sat with a glass of iced tea.

He slid in opposite her. "You got here fast."

"I was driving past when you called."

Edith returned with a second glass of tea. As soon as she had taken their order, Lexi nailed him with an eager gaze.

"Okay, we're here and pizza is on the way. So tell me what you learned."

"About two weeks before Kayla was killed, she told me that she got stopped by a cop in an unmarked vehicle. Of course, I didn't think anything of it at the time. She said that he insisted she'd made a turn and didn't signal, but she was positive she did. He supposedly ran her license, then told her he was going to let her go with a verbal warning."

Lexi's brows shot up. "Do you think he's our guy?"

"Possibly. I didn't make the connection until I stopped the Alcott boy for reckless driving. Knowing our killer is impersonating a cop, it got me thinking about Kayla."

"And?"

"According to Kayla, her tag and license were run, but the Florida Department of Law Enforcement has no record of it."

Lexi leaned forward in her seat, body tense with excitement. "Maybe he sees women who fit the description of what he's looking for, then stops them and pretends to run their license…"

He finished her thought. "And what he's really doing is taking note of their addresses. He stakes out the houses to make sure the women are alone, then abducts and murders them."

"We need to find out if any of the other victims

reported traffic stops by a cop in an unmarked vehicle. Are you busy the next few days?"

"Yep, but not too busy to fit in some phone calls and visits."

"Good. Because if this is what he's doing, we can use it to catch him." She took a long swig of her tea. "Kayla didn't happen to mention anything about him, did she? What he looked like? What agency he appeared to be with? Anything?"

He shook his head. "I've racked my brain trying to remember. If she mentioned anything, it's somewhere inside this thick skull of mine, buried deep."

She sat in silence, lips pursed. Then she brightened. "Well, I have a little information of my own. There's an orange grove next to the woods where Denise was found with some tire tracks going in. Looks like whoever made them left in a hurry, spun up quite a bit of dirt. Almost got stuck. Detectives recovered a ring."

"What kind of ring?"

"A class ring. Lake Region High School, class of 2002."

"Any distinguishing symbols or anything?"

"Yeah, ROTC."

"That narrows it down a bit."

"And," she added, "the stone is a garnet. Lake Region's colors are black, silver and blue, so my guess is the garnet is a birthstone."

"For?"

"January."

He nodded. "That narrows it down a lot."

"We're hoping the company that made the ring will be able to provide us with a name, if they keep records back that far."

"If not, just taking those in the 2002 graduating class who have January birthdays and were in ROTC should give us a workable number."

"I hope so. I'm ready for this to be over."

The heaviness in her tone shot straight to his heart. For five months she had been trying to catch this guy. Now, at the end of another long day, her expressive green eyes seemed to have lost some of their sparkle and the lines of her face reflected her fatigue.

He reached across the table and covered her hand with his own. "We're getting closer. At least now we have a live witness."

Edith approached and Lexi pulled her hand free. Moments later, a large mushroom, onion and pepperoni pizza sat on the table between them. After topping off their tea glasses, Edith left them alone again.

Alan pulled two steaming slices onto each of the plates. "So how's your mom?" He couldn't make the case be over. But maybe he could take her mind off of it while she ate.

She heaved a sigh. "Mom's just Mom. She sprained her ankle a couple of weeks ago, so I've been dropping by to help her with laundry and cleaning and stuff. But I get the distinct impression she's milking it."

Alan laughed. "That doesn't surprise me."

"She's getting to see me almost every day, so it's

given her some sense of control. I think if Mom had her way, she'd be orchestrating every detail of my life, right down to how many animals I have and what time I go to bed at night. I've always been her project, but it's worse since Dad died."

"At least you're not living under the same roof. So once the laundry or cleaning or whatever is finished, you get to walk away."

"Yeah, except she saw the press conference and ever since she's been insisting that I come and stay with her."

"It's not too often that I agree with your mother, but in this case, she's got a good point."

"I'd rather take my chances with a killer."

She stabbed a bite-size piece with a little more force than necessary. Maybe her mom wasn't a good topic of conversation.

For as long as he had known Lexi, there had been an amicable but defined tug-of-war between the two of them. There always seemed to be some sort of mild conflict—Lexi's annoyance when Patty laid out yet another path for her, and Patty's frustration when Lexi didn't follow it to a tee.

For the rest of the meal, he managed to steer the conversation away from both the case and Lexi's mother. After the leftover pizza had been split between two boxes, Lexi stood and gathered her purse from where it hung on the back of her chair. "I'll meet with you tomorrow morning. We've got a lot of phone calls to make."

"I'll have my dialing finger warmed up and ready."

She hooked her purse over her shoulder and began moving toward the door. "If we find out this is a link between the cases, we need to somehow get the word out to women in the twenty-to-twenty-five age group."

"And somehow keep the killer from knowing what we're doing."

"That's the hard part. If we go to the press, there's too good of a chance we'll tip him off."

He swung open the door and held it for her as an idea popped into his mind. He flashed Lexi a scheming smile. "Where can we find a lot of people in that age group all together?"

She returned his smile, her eyes widening. "College."

"We've got several in the county."

She nodded. "Polk State, Warner, Florida Southern, Southeastern…"

He continued laying out the plan. "We'll pass out flyers asking women to call if they get stopped by an officer but not ticketed. And we'll ask them to pass along the info to all of their friends."

"And if we get a lead, we'll stake out the girl's house and wait for the killer to strike."

He nodded, trying to ignore the vise that had suddenly clamped around his stomach. Somehow the thought of Lexi participating in a stake-out for a killer didn't sit well with him. But it was her job. She was trained for it, just as he was.

She pressed her key fob and the locks on the blue Mazda clicked open, accompanied by a beep. She turned to face him at the door. "But first we've got to find out whether the other victims had been stopped."

"And we'll start that tomorrow."

He smiled down at her. She seemed to stand a little straighter and anticipation had replaced the fatigue in her eyes.

Warmth spread through his chest and he fought back the urge to pull her into his arms. He would do anything to take some of the load off her.

Because no matter what happened, there would always be a soft spot in his heart where Lexi was concerned.

SEVEN

Palms rose skyward, fronds swaying in the gentle breeze. Beneath, wide walks stretched past beds filled with lush greenery and overflowing with color. Spring in Florida was always beautiful, but Southeastern University went all out.

Lexi fell in behind a group of students moving around the campus, talking and texting. She could be one of them, except for the uniform. And the pistol at her side.

For the past several days she and Alan had contacted friends and family members of the other victims. Three out of four of the women killed had mentioned getting pulled over and having their licenses run. And there was no record of any of the stops. So today she and Alan were hitting the colleges.

She removed her phone from her purse and pulled up a familiar number.

Alan answered on the third ring. "How's it going?"

"I'm finished. Just leaving Southeastern." She had

taken Winter Haven and Lakeland and given Alan the rest of the county. "How about you?"

"I'm headed to Webber. That's my last stop."

"Good."

"Everyone's been really cooperative. The office staff has promised to get the flyers into the hands of the professors to distribute to all the students. I've even had a couple offer to do all the copying."

"Same here. They're willing to do anything they can to help protect their students."

She looked down at the stack of pages she held. Help Us Catch a Killer stretched across the top of the page. Below that, the first paragraph revealed the same details the sheriff had given at the press conference. The second mentioned the traffic stops, with a request that anyone stopped and not ticketed by a cop in an unmarked vehicle call the number printed at the bottom. It was Lexi's cell phone number, something she'd had to fight Alan for. He had insisted that publicizing her number put her in unnecessary danger. She had insisted that it was her case, and if a young lady got stopped, she wanted to know any hour of the day or night. She'd won.

"Let me know when you finish at Webber." She slid into the driver's seat of her Mazda and closed the door. "After that, we wait and hope for our big break."

A beep sounded in her ear and she glanced at the display. "I've got a call coming through—352 area code."

"That's north of here."

Ocala. Her pulse picked up speed. Maybe Denise had remembered something else. She switched the call over.

"Hey, Lexi? It's Denise."

It was only four words, but the strength behind them surprised her. Denise no longer sounded like a petrified adolescent. The time spent in horse country was doing her good.

"I remembered something else. I don't know if it's important, but I wanted to let you know, just in case."

"That's great. Anything you can tell us might get us that much closer to catching this guy."

"Well, when he went to the trunk, I saw a piece of paper sitting in the console. It had a list of girls' names. Some of them were crossed out."

Her heart was pounding in earnest now. "Do you remember any of the names?"

"Lysandra."

"What?"

"Lysandra. *L-y-s-a-n-d-r-a.* I remember it because it's so unusual."

Lexi pulled a pen and pocket memo pad from her purse. "Tell me everything you can about this list, starting at the top."

"The first four or five names were crossed out."

"Do you remember any of them?"

A long stretch of silence passed before Denise finally answered. "Tiffany. Tiffany was one of the crossed-out names. And Amber. That's all I remember."

"You're doing great. How about the rest of the names?"

"Lysandra was next. Then Jeanie. There were two or three others, probably nine or ten names total, but I don't remember any of the others."

"Anything else you can remember?"

"No, that's all."

"You did great. That helps us a lot." If she had given them a list of Janes and Anns and Marys, they wouldn't have had any useful information. But Denise was right. Lysandra was an unusual name. Which greatly increased their chances of finding the killer's Lysandra.

Tonight Lexi would call Alan. Denise had told her at the hospital that the killer kept calling her Jeanie and saying that it wasn't her time yet. It wasn't her time yet, because Lysandra was supposed to be next. Or someone who represented Lysandra.

Tomorrow she would start a nationwide search of the name. Since the killer was choosing women between the ages of twenty and twenty-five and the offense happened ten years earlier, they were probably looking for someone in the thirty to thirty-five age range.

She dropped her phone into her purse and cranked up the car. As strains of Evanescence filled the confined space, her spirits lifted and she opened her mouth to sing along. It was the first real hope she'd had since learning that their Martin Jeffries lead was dead.

She pulled onto Longfellow belting out the notes, unable to tamp down the excitement.

If they could find this Lysandra, she could probably lead them to the killer.

Lexi slid the dish of tuna-and-noodle casserole into the oven and closed the door. Three sets of eyes watched her, and Suki let out another yowl.

"Okay, you're not going to starve before I get your food dished up. I promise."

The vocal Siamese responded with another indignant meow, while Midnight paced back and forth across the kitchen. Itsy lay in the corner, patiently waiting. Except her nondemanding pose was probably due more to laziness than patience.

Just as Lexi put the three dishes on the floor, the doorbell rang. Unease sifted over her, raising the hairs on the back of her neck. She didn't get a lot of visitors. At least unexpected ones. And the note from the killer, or someone posing as the killer, had put her a little on edge.

She tried to shake off the uneasiness. The note was probably nothing more than an idle threat, trying to scare her off the case. Or a prank. Besides, the killer didn't know where she lived. She hadn't had any traffic stops.

She moved through the foyer and checked the peephole. Prank or not, she wasn't unlocking the door without knowing who stood on her porch.

It was Alan. She swung open the door.

"What are you doing here?"

He flashed her a teasing smile. "You told me to let you know when I was finished at Webber."

"What I had in mind was a phone call."

"I also wanted to find out what you learned from Denise. And this was right on my way home. Sort of."

She backed away from the door to let him in.

"Mmm, something smells good."

"Tuna casserole."

He held up both hands. "Don't worry, I'm not going to invite myself for dinner."

"No, you're just going to drop hints and hope I will."

She walked into the kitchen and pulled two plates and glasses out of the cabinet. The company would be nice. Eating alone meal after meal sometimes got old. Besides, they had strategies to discuss.

Alan slid into one of the kitchen chairs. "So tell me what you learned from Denise. At least, I assume that was Denise who called."

"It was. It seems our killer is working off a list."

"What kind of list?"

"Girls' names. Denise saw it in the console the night he abducted her. She said the first four or five names were crossed off."

"I'm guessing it was five."

"Yeah, me, too, one for each of the girls killed. Then there were another four or five names that weren't crossed off yet."

"His remaining victims."

"Yep." She dropped a pot holder in the center of

the table and sat opposite him. "The next name on the list is Lysandra, then Jeanie."

Alan nodded slowly. "So we can probably assume Lysandra is next, or someone who represents Lysandra. Unless he deviates."

"My guess is he won't deviate again, especially after this last time. He almost got caught. Besides, he's too methodical."

The oven timer began to beep and she rose from the table. "That would be the dinner bell. You've probably figured out you're invited."

"Yeah, the second place setting sort of gave it away."

She took the casserole from the oven, and after putting a serving spoon into it, placed the dish in the center of the table.

Alan piled a spoonful onto each plate. "I'm so glad you didn't throw me out after letting me smell this for the past fifteen minutes. That would have been cruel."

"I wouldn't want to be accused of being cruel." She scooped a steaming mouthful onto her fork and blew on it. When she looked across the table at Alan, he was sitting with his head bowed. She raised her brows. He hadn't done that at Pappy's. Or maybe he had and she just hadn't noticed.

She waited until he opened his eyes and picked up his fork. "So when did you get religious?"

"About five and a half years ago. I had hit bottom, basically messed up my life. My personal life anyway.

I figured I could use some help straightening things out. At least not digging myself in deeper."

"Did it help?"

"It did. Praying for divine guidance in decisions makes all the difference in the world."

Maybe so. But it didn't take divine guidance to know that getting Lauren pregnant would be a bad idea. She could have told him that up front and saved him some heartache.

She scooped another bite onto her fork. "I'm glad it's working for you."

"It's for anyone who wants to accept it, you know."

Yeah, she knew that. Her parents hadn't taken her to church; her mom had been more into attending social events. But Lexi had occasionally gone with friends. And she'd actually listened. She'd liked the songs and the stories and the kindness of the people. She'd even prayed some. That was when she and God were still on speaking terms, before Prissy and Dad and Kayla.

"So what did you pray for?"

"Thanked God for the food, asked for help finding Kayla's killer." His eyes locked with hers and held. "Prayed for a chance to undo some past mistakes."

Her gaze fluttered to her plate. "There were mistakes on both ends. But it's all in the past." She once again met his eyes and offered him a weak smile. "Let's just leave it there. We have a case to solve."

Alan nodded, but there was reluctance in the motion. "So we have names. What next?"

"We do a nationwide search for women named Lysandra, then eliminate anyone over the age of forty and under the age of twenty-five."

"And we pay some Lysandras a visit."

"Or at least make some phone calls."

After seconds had been served and eaten, Alan stood to clear their empty plates. "Thanks for feeding me, even though I sort of invited myself. That wasn't my intent when I dropped by. The aroma sort of roped me in."

"No problem. It gave us a chance to bring each other up to speed on everything."

He stepped onto the porch. "Lock this door behind me."

"Believe me, I will."

As she watched him walk to his car, an unexpected longing rose up from within. And the past that she had successfully avoided all through dinner surged forward with a vengeance.

At one time, he was her life. She'd loved him with all her heart and had known without a doubt that they would someday commit to spending the rest of their lives together. Unfortunately, *someday* had arrived sooner for him than it had for her.

Now, six years later, *someday* seemed set off in some distant universe. Because regardless of what she felt for Alan, and no matter how desperately she longed for something more, nothing had changed.

Nothing had changed, yet everything had changed. Instead of leaving home for the first time, ready to experience long-awaited independence, she had become solidly set in her way of life—solitude, freedom, no one to consider except her cats.

Was she ready to give that up?

Would she ever be?

Alan laid aside the spy novel he had been reading and picked up the remote. He had checked out the movie lineup earlier and actually found something that spurred his interest.

It was another Friday night at home. What had once been a rare event was becoming a regular occurrence. But ever since Lexi had come back into his life, at least on a professional level, frequent casual dating didn't hold the appeal it once had. Besides, he didn't have the time. He was sort of working two jobs—official Harmony Grove police officer and unofficial Polk County Sheriff's Office assistant detective.

But he wasn't complaining. He was actually enjoying his dual role. Searching for clues. Uncovering the mystery one layer at a time. Working side by side with Lexi. The last was the most appealing of all.

The hours they were spending together had gone a long way toward mending shattered bridges. The long-term tension between them had all but dissipated, and during unguarded moments, slivers of emotion slipped past her defenses. He could see it in her eyes—signs of what had been there all those years ago. When this was over, maybe they could continue a relationship. Friendship, at least. But he hoped for more. Much more.

He clicked the remote and opening credits filled the screen. Soon other music mixed with the orchestral score streaming through the surround sound. Lexi was calling. He muted the volume on the TV.

A series of steady beeps came through the phone, followed by the thud of a door closing. She had apparently just gotten into her car. "Hey, I'm leaving Mom's. We had dinner together. Are you home?"

"Yeah."

"Alone?" The last word came out with a little hesitation.

"Yeah, I'm alone. What's up?"

"When Mom started getting overbearing, I excused myself, told her that you and I had some work to do on Kayla's case."

Alan smiled. Where Lexi's mother was concerned, a means of escape never hurt. "I'll be glad to help supply your getaway excuse. You want to stop by?"

"I'll be there in less than five minutes."

"What about the cats?"

"I took care of them before I went over to Mom's. So they're happy, fat and sassy."

When he opened the front door a few minutes later he stuttered a greeting. He was so used to seeing her in uniform, a weapon strapped to her hip, her hair pulled back in either a ponytail or a tight braid. Professional all the way.

But that wasn't who stood on his porch. This was

the old Lexi, relaxed and casual in a pair of snugly fitting jeans and a scoop-necked T-shirt. Her hair fell past her shoulders in wavy blond cascades, pressed in by previous hours in a braid.

His chest tightened and his thoughts flew back to other times she'd stood on that same porch, happy and in love. The memories left him with a keen ache and a hollow emptiness.

He swallowed hard and forced an easy smile. "Come in, and let's get started on that casework. We want to be able to tell your mother how we slaved away."

She returned his smile. Hers didn't seem to reflect any of the emotions that churned inside him.

He led her into the living room, where they each took a seat on the couch.

"Okay, tell me what you've got."

"We found the owner of the high school ring. Definitely a dead end. He works for Wilkins Irrigation. They do work there. A month or so ago, he got to the job on a Monday morning, realized he still had his ring on and took it off and put it in his pocket. When he got home, it was gone. So he figured it was lost for good. He was really happy to get it back."

"Did anyone check out his story?"

"Yep, Jim Wilkins himself says that the guy has worked for him for five years."

"How about Lysandra? Anything there?"

She opened the manila file folder she had carried in. "According to my search, there are five Lysandras in the U.S. that are between the ages of twenty-five and forty. I've eliminated three of them. One married right out of high school and is raising her five children with her farmer husband. Not likely to have been involved in anything that created a killer. But just in case, I called her anyway. She had a friend in grade school named Amber, who she lost contact with. She has an acquaintance named Jeanie, but doesn't know any Tiffanys. And she can't think of any circumstances where someone might be hurt or angry enough to want to take this kind of vengeance."

"What about the other two?"

"One's a marketing executive and one's a nurse. Neither of them had prior connections with the other names on the list. And like the first Lysandra, neither could think of anyone from their pasts who would have reason to do something like this."

"So we're striking out so far."

She flipped to another page in the folder. "There are still two left. Lysandra Yearwood is no longer at the job that shows up for her. We've got a home number, but haven't gotten an answer yet. And she apparently doesn't have a machine. Either that or it's turned off. We can try her again tonight."

She turned to the last page in the folder. "The fifth is a Lysandra Tucker. She went to Florida State for one year, stayed in one of the sorority houses. Then she got busted for drugs and dropped out of school. Never went back. She's thirty now, works as a bartender at a club over in Ybor City. And I get the distinct impression she's avoiding me."

"How so?"

"I've called three times over the past couple of days. Each time, the person who answered has told me to hang on, then comes back and says she's not available. I even called back when she was supposed to be on break."

"Interesting. You think she's hiding something?"

"It certainly appears that way." She pulled out her cell phone and pressed in the number, then put it on speaker phone.

"Club Dynamo, your place for a good time." The words were shouted over the music blasting in the background.

Lexi glanced at him and smiled. "May I please speak with Lysandra Tucker?"

"Who's calling, please?"

"Detective Alexis Simmons with the Polk County Sheriff's Office."

For several moments the only sound that came through the phone was the high-energy techno beat. The club employee's span of silence was just enough time to flash someone a questioning gaze and receive a silent answer.

"I'm sorry, she's not here tonight."

"How about if I call back tomorrow evening? Will she be working then?"

"Might be. I don't know for sure."

Lexi ended the call and gave him a conspiratorial wink. "How about a trip to Ybor tomorrow?"

"I'm game."

"This Lysandra isn't going to be able to avoid us very well if we're standing right in front of her."

"True. And how about Lysandra number four, Yearwood?"

Lexi referred back to the page in the folder, punched in a number and pressed the phone to her ear. Several seconds later her eyes widened and she sat up straighter.

Alan waited through the one-sided conversation. She was obviously getting further with this Lysandra than the last. Finally she ended the call.

"Well?"

"We've just eliminated our fourth Lysandra. Same basic story as the other three. But I'm putting all my hope on this last one. There's a reason she's avoiding us, and my guess is it has something to do with this case." She closed the folder and slid forward on the couch, preparing to stand.

"You want to watch a movie with me?" Of course, the movie he was planning to watch was already thirty minutes in. But for some reason, he wasn't ready for her to leave.

"I probably should go. It's been a long day."

He steeled himself against the disappointment filling his chest and walked her to the door. "You know you can drop by anytime. It doesn't have to be about the case." He grinned down at her. "Or escaping your mother."

"Thanks. But I don't want to bother you."

He rested his hand on the doorknob but didn't open the door. "You used to never worry about bothering me."

"Things were different then."

Yes, they had been. Did she feel the loss as acutely as he did at the moment? He couldn't tell. Her eyes were shielded, her emotions hidden behind the walls of professionalism.

He lifted a hand, determined to reach through those walls to the sweet, softhearted woman he had fallen in love with so long ago, and slid a finger along her jaw. "Why did you say no? Why wouldn't you marry me?"

"I was twenty-one and had never been away from home. I didn't think I was ready. The last thing I expected was to come back four months later and find you engaged to Lauren." Her eyes shifted to some point on the wall next to him. "It didn't take you long to replace me."

There was no bitterness in her tone, but the hurt that underlined her words sliced right through him.

"I had already gotten your message."

"What message?"

"The one you sent your mom to deliver."

Her gaze shifted back to his. Her eyes, no longer shielded, were filled with confusion. Uneasiness sifted over him, the sense that he was about to learn that he had made a huge, life-altering mistake.

He took a deep breath. "Before you left for school, you said we should date other people. I didn't want to, but I went along with it and did some casual dating. Every time I called you, you were heading to class or studying for an exam or had some other reason why you couldn't talk. I thought you were avoiding me. Then came the visit from your mom."

She stiffened and an icy hardness entered her gaze. Anger seemed to flow just beneath the surface, carefully held in check. "What did my mom say?"

"That you had met someone. That the two of you were quite serious, were even discussing marriage. She made it a point to tell me that he was studying to be a doctor and would be able to give you all the things you deserve."

The anger erupted, surging into the open as she clenched and unclenched her fists and stalked back into the living room. He followed her, and she spun and unleashed some of that fury on him. "And you believed her? You never once thought you should verify what she said with me?"

"I've known your mom is manipulative and controlling. But I've never known her to outright lie. She convinced me you didn't want to talk to me and that's why you sent her. And frankly, your actions hadn't exactly convinced me otherwise."

"I was busy. I was carrying a full load while working part-time." Her tone was defensive, but some of the fire had gone out of her. "I came back at Thanksgiving to tell you that I was ready, that if you were willing to wait until I finished school, I wanted to marry you."

A lead weight slid down his throat and settled in his gut. He had thought she had finally worked up the courage to dump him herself. And the last thing he had wanted was to hear the words from her own mouth. So he had shut her down by telling her he had moved on and was marrying Lauren.

"Oh, Lexi, I'm so sorry." He rested both hands on her shoulders, eyes pleading with her to understand. "I cared for Lauren, but I didn't love her. When she found out you had left me, she was right there, eager to step in, pushing for marriage. I knew you were the only one I would ever love. But since I would never have you, raising a child with Lauren didn't seem like such a bad second choice."

She looked up at him while he spoke, eyes once again veiled. Then she twisted from his grasp and bolted toward the front door.

He called after her, but she didn't turn back. She swung the door wide, leaped off the porch and flew down the short drive. Just before she slipped into the driver's seat of the Mazda, he caught a glimpse of her tear-streaked face. The sight tore his heart in two.

He closed the door and sagged against the wooden jamb.

Dear Lord, what have I done?

EIGHT

Lexi wiped at the tears streaming down her face. She hadn't only been betrayed by Alan. She had been betrayed by her own mother.

All her life, her mom had tried to make her into what she'd wanted her to be. And she had never quite succeeded. Because no matter how hard Lexi tried, she was never good enough.

But this time, her mother had crossed the line. She hadn't stuck with her usual control tactics—manipulating, cajoling, playing the guilt card. This time she'd resorted to deceit, an out-and-out lie.

And Alan, instead of talking to her, had believed the worst.

She wiped at the tears once more, determined to stop their flow. She would deal with her mother later. And Alan... Well, nothing had changed. He still had no excuse for sleeping with Lauren.

Up ahead, a brightly lit service station beckoned her. She wanted nothing more than to go home, curl up with her cats and have a good cry. But the light on her dash was warning her otherwise.

She stepped on the brake and pulled up to one of the pumps. While the gas poured into her tank, she leaned against the car and let her eyes drift down the street that ran alongside the station. A car sat some twenty yards away with only its parking lights on.

A sense of unease washed over her and the goose-flesh stood up on her arms. Had he followed her off the highway when she'd pulled into the station? She had been so upset, she hadn't paid attention. Distractions like that could get her killed. Especially now.

She finished pumping her gas and as she pulled back onto Highway 17, she cast frequent glances in her rearview mirror. Moments later, the car eased to a stop at the stop sign, then turned onto the main road.

Now she had no doubt. She was being followed. But she couldn't even identify the vehicle. It was too far back, nothing but a couple of headlights piercing the blackness of the cloudy night.

She slowed, allowing the other vehicle to catch up. But it slowed, too, maintaining the same distance. Another vehicle slipped between them.

She touched a button on her Bluetooth. "Call Tomlinson." Times like this made the voice-recognition feature a lifesaver. Literally.

She waited through two rings.

"Please answer." No way was she going to go home with someone following her. And no way was she going to pull over.

Relief washed over her at Tomlinson's warm greeting. She dispensed with the pleasantries.

"I'm being followed. The car is light, a four-door." That was as detailed as she could get. Whoever it was had been careful to park well out of the glow of the streetlights. All she had to go on was what she had seen in her rearview mirror those brief moments when he'd made his turn onto the highway. "I'm not sure, but it could be our guy."

"Give me your location."

"On 17, turning onto Winter Lake Road." She made several glances in her rearview mirror. The suspicious car turned, too. Now it was directly behind her but still hanging back, too far away to identify.

"Hold on. I'll get a couple units dispatched."

He didn't disconnect the call. Moments later, she heard him on the other line, spouting out directions.

Tomlinson came back on the phone. "You doing okay?"

"So far. I've made a right on Spirit Lake and he's still behind me. I think it might be a Toyota Camry, but I'm not sure." The light ahead turned red and she pressed the brake. "I hope our people get here fast."

"They're being dispatched now."

By the time she braked to a stop, the light had turned green again. She accelerated through the intersection. But the car didn't follow. Instead, it veered into a squealing right turn, as if having had a sudden change of plans.

"He just turned right on Coleman." She braked for a hard right onto Seventh Street, then made the one-block jaunt to continue down Coleman. But the light-colored Camry, or whatever it was, was long gone.

Why had he suddenly given up the pursuit? It was almost as if he'd been listening to a police scanner.

She couldn't rule it out. If he had a strobe light, he could certainly have a police scanner.

She heaved a sigh. "I lost him. I think he cut through one of the subdivisions off Hatfield. He knew we were on to him."

She disconnected the call and during the final miles home, her heart rate gradually returned to normal. That was close. She had to remain more alert. No matter what happened, she needed to be constantly aware of her surroundings. She had let down her guard, just for a few minutes. If she hadn't stopped for gas, she might have led the killer right to her home.

Before pulling into her driveway, she scanned the street in front and behind her. She was alone—no strange cars, no distant headlights. She pulled the Mazda into the double carport next to her sheriff's vehicle, and for the first time ever wished she had a garage instead. Auburndale was small. If someone really wanted to find her, it wouldn't be that difficult.

When she opened the front door, Suki met her in the foyer, loudly berating her for leaving. And when she headed toward the kitchen for a drink of water, the cat almost plowed her over getting there.

"Look, I already fed you." She bent to pick up the talkative Siamese and the meows immediately turned to purrs. "Just because someone comes to the kitchen doesn't mean it's time to eat again."

She drank the glass of water, then walked into the living room. It was too early to go to bed. And she didn't feel like watching something on TV. She didn't want to read, either.

Tomorrow she would be spending the afternoon with Alan. There was no way around it. She had already invited him on her investigative trip to Ybor City. And there would likely be plenty more shared excursions before this was all over. She needed to just buck up and forget about what they'd had in the past.

She heaved a sigh and let her gaze circle the room. The old spinet in the corner called to her. Two months after moving in, she had found it at a yard sale for fifty bucks. The seller had even moved it for her.

She sank onto the bench and ran her hand over the keys. Her skill on the piano was a gift from her mother. But it wasn't until recently that she considered it so. As a child, she had sat through endless piano lessons and spent countless hours practicing and participating in contests and recitals. And hated every minute of it. Playing the piano had always been her mother's passion, not her own.

Now she took comfort in the activity. There was no one to tell her she had to practice, no impossible standard to live up to, no pressure to perform.

She put her hands on the keyboard and started to play Beethoven's "Für Elise." Her fingers glided over the keys and she closed her eyes, letting the emotion of the piece swell inside her. The tinkling melody filled the room and circled around her, soothing her frayed nerves. She would never tour the world as a concert pianist. She had no desire to. Playing for her own enjoyment was more than enough.

All the glitz and glamour was her mother's dream. And she might have achieved it if she hadn't met and married Lexi's father. She had given up a lot for love. And regretted it ever since.

Lexi's eyes flew open and her hands hung suspended over the keys, Beethoven suddenly silenced. All her life, she'd thought her mother was trying to make her into what she'd wanted her to be. She'd been wrong. Her mother was trying to make her into what she wished she herself had become.

Always trying to live her dreams through someone else.

Patty Simmons regretted never pursuing her dream of being in the spotlight, praised for her talent, loved by thousands. So she'd forced that dream on her daughter.

And she regretted not marrying into wealth. So when she saw Lexi about to make the same "mistake," committing her future to a lowly police officer, she stepped in and took action. And ruined two lives in the process. Three, counting Lauren's.

All her life her mother had gotten her way, cajoled and manipulated others to do her bidding. And when that hadn't worked, she'd turned to deceit and outright lies.

Lexi and Alan had played right into her hands.

And they were still playing into her hands. Lexi didn't want to give up her independence, her right to make her own decisions. But in a sense, she already had. Because as long as she kept pushing Alan away, she was letting her mother continue to wield her control.

She shook her head and released a heavy sigh. It was way too complicated. And tonight she was too tired to try to sort it all out.

Once again, she lowered her hands to the keyboard and began to play.

The small wooden building stood hemmed in between a tattoo parlor and a nail salon, little more than a hole in the wall. Music pulsed through the closed door and neon in the windows enticed patrons with a promise of the booze they would find inside. Across the mansard, more neon flashed the words Club Dynamo. Or more accurately, Club Dyna, since the last third of the word wasn't lit.

Alan swung open the wooden door and paused, steeling himself against the onslaught to his senses. Lights strobed, reflecting off the smoke curling through the air, and the music, now unobstructed, reverberated through his rib cage.

Lexi leaned into him. "We should have come armed with earplugs."

"Not a bad idea." His voice was several decibels

louder than normal. How people conversed in settings such as this, he'd never understand.

He wound his way toward the bar, past a dance floor filled to capacity with writhing bodies, then climbed onto a bar stool. Lexi took one next to him and laid a manila folder on the counter in front of her. Two bartenders moved back and forth, filling drink orders and chatting with patrons. One was blond, petite and pretty. And much too young to be their Lysandra. Likely a USF student, taking on the weekend shift to work her way through school.

The other was older and tougher looking, lacking the youthful innocence of the blonde. Her jet-black hair was cut short in a jagged, chopped style and highlighted with streaks of purple. Some kind of hair gel stiffened the uneven clumps, accentuating the unconventional cut.

Lexi nodded toward the older bartender and put her mouth close to Alan's ear. "You think that's our Lysandra?"

"I'm almost positive."

The blonde looked over at them and held up a finger. After setting two drinks in front of a couple of ladies at the other end of the bar, she hurried in their direction.

"What can I get you folks?"

He smiled up at her. "Not that I don't like you, but I was hoping to be served by Lysandra."

"Not a problem." She turned and shouted to her coworker halfway down the bar. "San, this one's yours."

Lysandra's gaze drifted over the other patrons and came to rest on Alan. The friendly smile she had for her customers widened and she closed the distance between them. Even in the poor lighting, at close range, the heavy makeup did nothing to hide the creases that surrounded her mouth and marked the edges of her eyes. If she was thirty, those were some hard thirty years.

She stopped in front of him and leaned on the bar, mouth curved upward in invitation. "Hey, big boy, what can I get you?"

Lexi tensed next to him, almost imperceptibly. It might even have been his imagination. But he wasn't imaging the prickly vibes she was sending out now. Maybe she felt something for him after all.

But this wasn't the time to explore possibilities. They had finally found the elusive Lysandra. Now to get her to talk.

He returned her smile. "A Coke, and the same for the lady."

One side of her mouth rose a little higher. "The hard stuff. Be back in a sec."

She returned to set a glass in front of each of them.

Alan smiled up at her again. "You're a hard lady to get hold of."

"If I'd have known you were trying, I'd have made it a little easier." She ran a painted nail along the back of one of his hands. Something told him she wouldn't be nearly as friendly if he was in uniform.

He resisted the urge to pull his hand away. Shallow

flirtiness had never appealed to him. Lexi's genuine air was so much more refreshing. "My friend here has tried for the past three days to reach you, with no success. If I didn't know better, I'd think you were trying to avoid us."

She pulled away from the counter, back ramrod-straight and green eyes guarded. Distrust flashed in their depths, pushing aside all hint of the invitation that was there only moments earlier. She crossed her arms in front of her. "Jake's trying to pin everything on me, isn't he? Well, it's not going to work, because I wasn't there. I figured out he was trouble and was going to pull me down with him, so I dumped him."

Alan nodded. "That was a wise choice. But Jake isn't the reason we're here."

Her eyes widened slightly, but she didn't speak.

Lexi went on to explain. "We have a serial killer stalking young women in Polk County. We're pretty sure what he's doing is retribution for something that happened ten years earlier. We have some names of the women who were involved. One, of course, is Lysandra. There was also Amber, Tiffany and Jeanie."

Recognition flitted across her features. She knew the names. But she shook her head.

"I'm sorry. I can't help you."

"Look," Lexi continued, "we just need to ask you a few questions, see what you can remember."

Lysandra shook her head again. "I'm sorry, I don't know any women by those names."

Alan studied her. She was lying, and he knew it.

He fished through the folder and pulled out a photo of the first victim. It wasn't one of the earlier ones, with nothing more than some minor bruising. It was the last one, head cocked unnaturally to the side, bulging, lifeless eyes, discolored face and ugly brownish-red ring around the neck. This time he *was* going for shock value.

He slammed the photo face up on the counter. "Look, lady, young women are dying, and you might be able to stop it."

Her gaze fell on the picture but didn't stay there long. A nanosecond later she jerked away, lips turned out in revulsion. For several moments she stood, indecision set in her features.

Finally she cast a glance at her coworker. "Cover for me."

After she came out from around the counter, she led them to a table in the corner, farthest from the massive speakers pumping their racket onto the dance floor. Not that it helped. There was probably no peace and quiet to be had within a three-block radius.

Lysandra slid into a chair, her expression somber. "Amber, Tiffany and Jeanie—we were all in the same sorority at Florida State."

Lexi nodded. "Anyone you can think of who might have had a bone to pick with you ladies?"

Lysandra gave a dry laugh. "Yeah, a whole bunch of guys. Where do you want to start?"

"How about the why? Then we'll get to the who."

"It was all part of joining."

"What was?" Alan asked.

"Using our feminine wiles to lure a guy into a really embarrassing situation."

He nodded. Hazing was illegal. But that didn't stop it from happening. Not by a long shot. "Do you remember the names of any of these guys?"

Lysandra thought for a moment. "Frank. I remember him, because he's the one I set up."

"What was Frank's last name?"

"Thompson or Thomas, maybe Tomlin. I'm not good with names."

Lexi made some notes on a blank sheet of paper in her folder. "Any others you can remember?"

"No, that's it."

Lexi continued, "So one of the requirements of getting into the sorority was to lure some unsuspecting guy into a compromising position. Then what?"

"Then we took pictures and plastered them all over campus. So the guys got a lot of ribbing."

Alan's pulse picked up and he cast Lexi a meaningful glance. The killer's photos weren't trophies. They already knew that. But they weren't for the purpose of publicity, either. They were for revenge. His tormenters had photographed him at his worst, so he photographed his victims at theirs.

He shifted his gaze back to Lysandra. "Any of those guys seem especially upset over your pranks?"

Lysandra shrugged. "Most of them took it in stride."

"Most, but not all?"

For several moments Lysandra stared down at her

hands clasped on the table. When her gaze again met his, it was intense, as if she had suddenly realized the import of what she had participated in.

She nodded slowly. "There was one. He didn't laugh it off like the others."

"How so?" Lexi asked.

"He was really angry, not like an explosive, blow-up-and-get-violent anger. More like a seething, beneath-the-surface anger that would simmer and stew until it would one day come out, cold and lethal. I avoided him as much as I could, because after that, he scared me. Any time we would pass each other on campus, he would stare me down." An involuntary shudder shook her shoulders. "That was the last time I had any part in the hazing pranks."

Lexi took a swig of her Coke. "Do you remember his name?"

Lysandra closed her eyes, her brows pulled together in concentration. "Gary, maybe? I don't remember for sure, but I think it was Gary." She shook her head. "I can't believe he's killing people over this."

She once again lowered her gaze to her hands. "A few months after this, I was gang raped. I figured it was retribution for all the bad stuff I had done over my life. You know, karma." Her gaze fluttered back up to meet Lexi's. "I thought I had paid my dues, but apparently not."

Lexi reached across the table and put her hand over Lysandra's. "Don't blame yourself. These deaths are the responsibility of the killer and no one else.

But we're asking you to help us catch him, before he kills again."

"Tell me what I can do."

"Give us the names of all your sisters who had any involvement in Gary's prank."

"There were about ten of us. I can give you the names, but I've lost touch with all of them. I only went to Florida State for a year."

Yeah, they knew that. And they knew why. But there was no sense bringing it up now.

Lexi continued, "Do you have any photos?"

"Not of Gary. I think I still have some of my friends."

"Can we see them?"

Lysandra nodded. "I live only two blocks from here. Let me get Josie to cover a few more minutes. Then I've got to get back to work."

Alan followed Lysandra and Lexi out the door. This had been their most productive day yet. Not only did they have a motive, but they also had a first name.

And maybe somewhere in all that college memorabilia, there would be a photo that Lysandra had forgotten about.

A photo of Gary.

NINE

Lexi followed Lysandra down the sidewalk, thankful for Alan's presence next to her. The neighborhood seemed a little on the rough side, with trash on the edges of the street and bars on most of the windows.

But Lysandra didn't seem to mind. She walked along at a good clip, chatting as she went.

"I stuck everything from my college days in a box and have lugged it with me everywhere I've gone."

Lexi smiled. That box had probably gone through a lot of lugging. Hopefully its contents would prove valuable.

"It's tucked away in the top of the closet. I haven't been through it in forever. I'm not even sure why I keep all that old stuff."

She veered off the sidewalk and headed toward a narrow wrought iron stairway that hugged the side of a chipped stucco building. At the top, she put the key into the lock and swung the door wide.

"Well, this is home. It's not great, but it's all I could

afford when I left Jake. I've come to the conclusion that sometimes it's better to be alone."

She led them into the apartment and closed the door behind them. Fresh paint covered sections of missing plaster that had never been repaired, but the place was neat and tidy.

"So are you guys together?" Lysandra flung the question over her shoulder as she headed toward the bedroom.

Lexi followed but stopped in the doorway. "Yes and no. We work for separate departments, but we're working together on this case."

"No, I meant, are you a couple?" She turned to face them, her gaze shifting from Lexi to Alan and back to Lexi again. "You look like you belong together. There's good energy between you."

Lexi opened her mouth to respond, but Lysandra was already wrestling a box down from the shelf in the closet. She plopped it on the bed and pulled back the flaps. A Seminoles pennant lay across the top. Beneath it were a couple of shoe boxes, along with a mug, a blanket and some other FSU memorabilia.

"All the pictures are in these two boxes." She took the lid off one and pulled out a thick stack of photos. After thumbing through several of them, she handed one to Lexi. "This is Amber."

Lexi showed the photo to Alan. "Stephanie."

Lysandra looked up from the pictures she held. "Who?"

"Stephanie Wilson, the third victim. Amber resembles her. Or I should say, Stephanie resembled Amber."

Lexi held on to the photo, and Lysandra flipped through several more pictures.

"Here's one of Amber and Tiffany together."

"Do you have a close-up of Tiffany?"

"Probably." She sat on the bed and continued going through the photos until she had sorted all of them from the first box. After stuffing several handfuls back into the box, she handed the remaining pictures to Lexi.

"These are the ones you'd be interested in." Lysandra moved to stand next to her. "That's Tiffany, more close up."

Lexi showed the picture to Alan.

"Donna Jackson?"

She nodded. Tiffany's face was a little more rounded than Donna's, but the resemblance was definitely there. Similar build, same wavy, shoulder-length hair, deep brunette.

By the time Lysandra finished taking them through the stack of photos, they had linked five of her friends to the five victims. A sixth, Jeanie, could have passed for Denise's sister.

Lysandra sat back on the bed and removed the lid from the other box. "I'll check the others."

Midway through, she suddenly stopped. "Gary. I didn't know I still had this. All the others went up around campus."

Lexi's pulse jumped to double time and she moved to see what Lysandra held. Her eyes widened. "How in the world...?"

"Bridgett did it."

Bridgett, represented by Meagan Bowers, victim number one. She must have been incredibly persuasive, because she had somehow convinced Gary to dress in nothing but a T-shirt and a pink tutu.

The problem was, he was running away from the camera. So all they had to go on was some longish brown hair, a white T-shirt thinly concealing a bony back, and a tulle-covered rear end.

Lysandra sighed. "It was quite a feat. The hard part was sneaking him past our house mom. The rest was easy. Bridgett promised him a great party, lots of booze and wild, beautiful women. But she told him that to be initiated in as one of our fun party guys, he had to let go of all his inhibitions. And putting on that pink tutu was what he had to do to prove it. When he came out of the bathroom and Bridgett led him into the rec room, we were waiting for him...with cameras and lots of laughter."

But Lysandra wasn't laughing now. In fact, she looked as though she was going to be sick. And Lexi couldn't blame her. Their silly pranks had created a killer. He had started with Bridgett, the orchestrator of his humiliation, and was methodically working his way through each of her friends.

Except the women paying the price were innocent,

their only crime being unfortunate enough to resemble his tormenters.

Lysandra shook her head. "I had no idea."

Lexi placed a comforting hand on her shoulder. "I know you didn't. None of you had any way of knowing something like this would happen."

"I wish I could take it back. I'd do anything to go back and relive that year."

Lexi let her hand fall from Lysandra's shoulder. "Can we take these? We'll make copies and send them back, if you give us a mailing address."

Lysandra nodded and began to repack the unneeded photos.

Alan held up a hand. "Before you put all those back, do you have any pictures of yourself?"

"Yeah, I think I do." She began fishing through the boxes, talking while she searched. "I actually looked a lot different then. This isn't my natural hair color." She gave a short laugh. "Obviously the purple isn't natural. But the black isn't, either. My true hair color is a mousy brown, sort of like that dresser over there." She tilted her head toward the other side of the room. "In college, though, I was a platinum blonde. Ah, here's one."

She handed the photo to Alan, and his complexion seemed to grow several shades paler. He lifted his gaze to Lexi's, and the fear she saw there sent tiny shards of apprehension spiking through her. She really didn't want to know, but she moved closer anyway, eyes seeking what he held.

Apprehension morphed to dread. As expected, the girl in the photo was blond, hair straight and silky, just past shoulder length. Much like Lexi's own.

Lysandra's voice cut across her thoughts.

"I hadn't noticed before, but you and I could almost be sisters." She gave a nervous laugh. "You wouldn't happen to be adopted, would you? I am."

Lexi shook her head. "No, I'm not. But maybe we're distant cousins."

By the time Lysandra walked them to the front door, they had a good handful of photos, with the subjects identified on the backs by first and last names.

"We can walk back together." Lysandra pulled a key from her pocket and opened the door. "If I don't get back soon, Josie is going to string me up."

When they got back to Club Dynamo, Lexi stopped at the door. There was no reason to endure the assault to her eardrums or her lungs.

"Thanks for talking to us." She gave Lysandra an encouraging smile. "You were a big help."

"No problem. I'm happy to help in any way I can. If there's anything else I can do, anything at all, let me know. I'm afraid I won't live long enough to atone for my part in this."

"And you don't have to." It was Alan who spoke. "You're carrying an awful lot of guilt. God's forgiveness is there for the asking. But you'll also have to learn to forgive yourself."

Lysandra gave a brief dip of her head and disappeared inside. As Lexi walked with Alan to his car, an unexpected warmth filled her chest. Alan's compassion and tenderness were two of the reasons she had fallen in love with him. That, along with his integrity and sense of justice. Those boyish good looks hadn't hurt him any, either.

Now, at thirty-two, his looks were no longer boyish. Fine lines, visible only when he smiled, fanned out from the corner of each eye, and his dark hair, which had previously been a little on the long side, was cut in a close, layered style that tamed the natural curl.

But the good looks were definitely still there. Enough to turn female heads. Lysandra's included.

Lexi slid into the passenger seat of the Mustang and waited for Alan to get in. "She ended up being a whole lot more helpful than I anticipated."

"Yeah. I was pleasantly surprised."

"I wasn't sure how things were going to go at first. Sitting at the bar there, I was beginning to think you had acquired a new girlfriend. She acted like she could hardly keep her hands off you."

He grinned over at her. "You jealous?"

Lexi rolled her eyes. "Not hardly." She reached for her seat belt and clicked it into place. "But our conversation last night did get me thinking."

His brows shot up and a cautious hope crept into his eyes. "Oh?"

She laid her head back against the seat and stared through the windshield. "We let her win. She doesn't deserve that."

Alan didn't respond. He would know who she was talking about. She didn't have to explain.

"For six years, we've played right into her hands. But she's still not happy, because I'm not married to a disgustingly wealthy corporate executive or touring the world, wowing millions with my musical brilliance. But as long as I'm single, I don't think she'll ever give up trying."

Alan started the car but made no move to back from the parking space. "So what do you have in mind?"

Actually, she didn't know. She certainly wasn't ready to accept that ring she'd rejected so many years ago.

"Do you still care for me?" His voice was soft.

Lexi could feel his eyes on her, his inquisitive gaze boring into her. "It's not that simple."

He leaned back against the seat with a sigh. "Because of Lauren."

"Lauren is just part of the problem."

"Lauren was the biggest mistake of my life. She came to me in trouble, pregnant and alone. And I let my kindhearted nature get in the way of good sense. Besides, at the time, I didn't feel I had anything to lose." He reached across to cover her hand resting in her lap. "I thought I had already lost what was dearest to me—your love."

His palm was warm against the back of her hand, his touch comforting. But inside, her mind was whirling. Had she heard him right?

She turned to look at him. "Lauren was pregnant when she came to you?"

"Yes. Otherwise we would have waited and that ill-fated wedding would never have taken place."

"So the baby wasn't yours."

He pulled his hand back suddenly. "Of course not! She was almost two months along when we started seeing each other. I took her out several times, more as a friend offering encouragement and support. But when I told her about your mom's visit, that was when she really ramped up her pursuit. Next thing I knew, we were shopping for a ring. She instigated it, but I went along with it. And I've regretted it ever since. Even more so since working with you."

"So what happened?"

"A month after marrying, she had a miscarriage. She didn't need me anymore and took off. As much as I hate to admit it, I was almost relieved when she left. We never loved each other. She was using me, and I still loved you."

Lexi shook her head, trying to wrap her mind around what she had just learned. Lauren was already pregnant. Alan wasn't sleeping around while she was at school.

His eyes were still on her. "So where do we go from here?"

She took a deep breath and turned to look at him. "How about we start over and take it slow?" She cared for him. Maybe even still loved him. But she had a lot more thinking to do before she was ready to cast aside her independence.

A warm smile crept up his cheeks and her stomach did a little flip.

"All right. I won't push. We'll take it slow." He leaned across the console and pressed his lips to her forehead.

She closed her eyes, relishing the sensation of his warm breath against her face.

Slow was going to be difficult. Because at the moment she wanted nothing more than for him to wrap her in his arms and kiss her fully and deeply.

The way he used to.

Alan strolled along the winding walks of Harmony Grove Park, Lexi's hand in his. Curved beds hugged the edges of the wide concrete path that circled the fountain up ahead. Sometime in the distant past, the ladies of the Harmony Grove Garden Club had taken over responsibility of those beds. Now it seemed their goal each spring was to outdo what they had accomplished the prior year. Lush greenery formed a dramatic backdrop for blooms in every color of the palette, not leaving a single square inch of any bed bare.

He led Lexi around the fountain and toward the lake at the west end of the park. He couldn't get her to accompany him to church, but she had agreed to meet him for a picnic in the park afterward. And the weather couldn't have been better if it had been custom ordered. A balmy seventy-eight degrees under a sunny blue sky with just a spattering of fluffy white clouds. Now, with a belly full of chicken and potato salad and a heart overflowing with contentment, life seemed exceptionally sweet.

After walking only one-third of the two-mile perimeter of the lake, Lexi stopped in front of a bench shaded by a huge oak. She smiled up at him, lips touched with some pinkish-colored gloss, reapplied after lunch. Lexi never was one for heavy makeup. She didn't need it. With her soft features, she possessed a clean, natural beauty.

"Do you know where we are right now?"

He raised his brows. "We're at the park."

She sat on the bench, pulling him down with her. "I know, but do you know what's significant about this exact spot?"

He looked out toward the lake, where a pair of mallard ducks were gliding on the surface a short distance away, and tried to jog his memory. It wasn't where he'd asked her to marry him. That had happened on the front porch of her house, with the two of them sitting on the swing.

She hadn't taken the ring. Instead, she'd jumped to her feet and started rambling about how she was leaving for school, and that it wasn't fair for her to tie him down and expect him to wait for her, and how they both needed to be free to date other people. He had left that evening with a lump in his throat and a hole in his heart.

But he wasn't going to think about that. Now he was with her, and God was possibly giving them a second chance.

"No, what's significant about this spot?"

"This is where you kissed me for the first time."

He grinned down at her. "Are you sure about that?"

"Positive. It was after the Memorial Day cookout. We had just finished watching fireworks and were walking around the lake. And you stopped right here and kissed me."

"Then you're right. It *is* a special place." He released her hand to wrap his arm around her and pull her to his side. The memory she brought up stirred something in him, carrying him back to those early days, when love was new and the future was bright with promise. Would it be even sweeter the second time around?

He had promised her he would take it slow. But how slow was slow? He could really use some clarification. Because he was so ready for a replay of that first kiss.

He cleared his throat and reined in his thoughts. His safest bet was to let her set the pace. When she was ready, he would know. At least that was what he hoped.

She sighed and stretched out her legs in front of her, crossing them at the ankles. "You know, after Dad died, I used to come down here a lot. Mom thought I had gone back home, but I was right here, sitting, staring out at the lake, trying to find answers."

"Did you ever find any?"

"Nope, never did."

"If the question is why, sometimes the answer doesn't come until after this life is over. God sees the big picture, and we just have to trust Him to get us through the rough places."

"I have a hard time serving a God who allows so much evil in the world."

He smiled over at her, his tone gentle. "You don't want anyone to try to control you, but you're expecting God to do just that."

"What do you mean?"

"He created us with free will. Evil is never part of His plan, but He allows us to make our own choices, even if those choices hurt ourselves and others. God didn't create us to be a bunch of puppets."

She heaved a sigh and seemed to sag against him. "I'm just tired of people dying."

The sadness in her tone stabbed through him and he pulled her closer, longing to somehow soothe away her pain. It wasn't just Prissy and Kayla and her father. There were countless others she had encountered whose lives had been snuffed out before their time. Being a homicide detective had to wear a person down, especially someone as compassionate as Lexi.

She hiked up her shoulders, then let them fall, as if shaking off the melancholy that had descended on her. Lexi was compassionate, but she was also strong, and she wouldn't let herself wallow in sadness for long.

She pushed herself to her feet to continue her

course around the lake. When they reached his car, he turned to face her. "How about taking in a movie with me?"

She gave him an apologetic smile. "I think I'm going to pass. As much as I've enjoyed our outing, I should probably be getting home."

Disappointment washed over him. "Already?"

"I wanted to run the names Lysandra gave us through the database. If we can talk to her friends, maybe one of them will remember Gary's full name."

"Can't you just goof off this afternoon? Even God took a day off. He spent six days creating the world, then rested on the seventh."

"I can't take a day off as long as women are dying."

Yeah, she would look at things that way. He opened the passenger door for her to slide into the seat. "Anything I can help with?"

"Not tonight. When I get some addresses and phone numbers, I'll have you help me contact them."

A few minutes later he braked to a stop in his driveway, right next to the blue Mazda. He had wanted to pick her up, but she had insisted on meeting him, saying she needed to check on her mother anyway.

So now she was getting ready to drive home. Alone.

"How about if I follow you?"

She leaned back against her car and smiled up at him. "That's not necessary. I'll be fine."

He stepped closer. There was more he wanted to say. But he had been putting it off, because he knew it would be a point of contention between them. They could discuss it all day long and probably never agree.

But he had to try to talk some sense into her.

"Lexi, you're the spitting image of the young Lysandra."

She tensed. "I know. I saw the photo the same time you did."

He ignored the annoyance in her tone. "What if the killer has realized that fact, too?"

"I'm being careful."

"I know you are. But I'm worried about you. Ever since I saw that picture, I haven't been able to get it out of my mind."

Her gaze softened and she reached up to put both of her hands on his cheeks. "My job has its risks. If we're going to make this work, you're going to have to accept that and trust me to make the right decisions."

"All right." He gave a small nod and she lowered her hands. He should probably step back and give her some space. But he couldn't get his feet to obey.

And she didn't seem to be in any more of a hurry to leave than he was to let her leave. She stood staring up at him, gaze warm and lips slightly parted. A fresh, clean fragrance drifted to him, some kind of lavender-scented hand lotion or body wash, the same scent that had teased him off and on at intervals throughout the afternoon.

What would she do if he kissed her? He had refrained all afternoon. Was that slow enough?

Maybe so. Because the next moment she stood on

her tiptoes and brushed a soft kiss across his lips. "Look, I'll call when I get home. I promise."

He stood frozen, fighting for control, afraid that if he moved he would crush her to him and kiss her back. And it wouldn't be a sweet, casual peck. Finally he stepped away and forced a smile.

"All right. If I don't hear from you within thirty minutes, I'm sending out the search parties."

As he watched her back out of the drive and start up the road, his heart clenched. Somewhere out there was a killer. And Lexi was vulnerable. After six long years, he was so close to winning her back. He couldn't lose her again.

Lord, please protect her.

Her taillights disappeared from view and he turned to walk into the house. His recliner beckoned, but he didn't bother to settle into it. There was no way he could sit still. Instead he began to pace the living room. If only she would go stay with her mom. Or take in a roommate. Or let him sleep on the couch.

But he knew Lexi. And she would do none of those things. She was far too independent. There was nothing he could do.

Actually, there was something he could do. He stopped pacing and pulled out his phone. Maybe she wouldn't let anyone stay with her. But she couldn't stop people from checking on her.

He punched in a now familiar number. Tomlinson answered on the first ring.

"Hi, Sarge, it's Alan White."

"Is Lexi all right?"

"She's fine right now. But I was wondering if you could have some units drive by her place on a regular basis and check on her. I'm worried about her."

"Is something going on that I need to know about?" His tone was heavy with suspicion.

"Yeah, we found Lysandra and talked to her. I'll let Lexi fill you in on the details. But we're pretty sure that the next victim is going to be someone who looks like Lysandra did ten years ago."

"What's that got to do with Lexi?"

"Ask her to show you Lysandra's picture. She and Lexi could be sisters."

"Oh, that's not good." Tomlinson was concerned. Alan didn't need to see the worried frown or creased brow. It all came through the phone.

"Lexi isn't going to back down. And though I don't agree with her, I understand. She's determined to find her cousin's killer and doesn't want to leave it in someone else's hands."

"Kayla Douglas was Lexi's cousin?"

Uh-oh, he had said too much. "Please don't tell her I told you. I just wanted to let you know what kind of danger she's in so everyone can be watching out for her."

"We'll do that. Thanks for letting me know, son."

Alan ended the call and laid his phone on the end table. Conflicting emotions churned in his gut—relief that other deputies would be watching out for her, and fear that she would find out he talked to Tomlinson.

And regret. Because he had no doubt that she *would* learn of the conversation. And when she did, she would be furious.

Whatever walls had come down over the past two days would go right back up.

And she would be lost to him all over again.

TEN

Lexi stood at the watercooler, watching the ice-cold water slowly fill her thirty-two-ounce 7-Eleven mug. Ever since that morning's briefing, she had been holed up in her cubicle, searching databases, poring over names, trying to gather contact information. She was getting closer. She had already made contact with two of Lysandra's friends. She had the contact information of three others, but hadn't yet had any luck getting hold of them. The last four were still at large.

She released the lever to stop the flow of water and took a long swig. It wasn't until she turned that she realized a line had formed behind her. A line of one anyway.

She smiled up at Greg, the newest detective in the unit. "Sorry. I didn't mean to hog the watercooler." She stepped aside. "Help yourself."

"No problem. I'm not in that big of a hurry." He moved his cup to his left hand, then held out his right. "I don't think we've been properly introduced. Greg Morganson."

She took his extended hand. "Lexi Simmons."

"I'm pleased to meet you, Lexi. I've heard a lot of good things about you. You're well respected."

"Thanks."

She turned and walked back to her cubicle, leaving Greg filling his cup. He was being friendly, and she hoped she came across as being friendly back. But she wasn't there to socialize, she was there to work. And as long as she held that attitude, it would keep her out of trouble. She wasn't sure which was worse, office politics or office romance. She avoided both.

She had just settled in at her desk when a large figure filled the opening to her cubicle. Tomlinson might be close to retirement age, but he hadn't lost any of his bulk.

She smiled up at him. "How's it going?"

"Can I see you in my office?"

It was phrased as a question, but she had no doubt. It was a command, not a request.

She sprang to her feet and followed him past a stretch of cubicles to one of the offices at the edge of the bay. Whatever he had to say, he wanted more privacy than what the cubicles offered. That by itself didn't concern her. His stern manner did. A thread of uneasiness slid through her mind.

He closed the door behind her, then motioned toward one of the two chairs that faced his desk. "Have a seat."

Once he had settled into the padded office chair, he

leaned back, fingers intertwined over his abdomen. "So how did your trip to Ybor go?"

"Very productive. We have a first name. And we have a picture. Unfortunately, it's from the back. So all we know about him is that he has brown hair and is thin, or was at the time. And he doesn't look good in pink tulle."

Tomlinson cocked a brow at her.

"It's a long story. Anyway, five of her friends bear a strong resemblance to the five victims, and a sixth looks a lot like Denise."

"And what about Lysandra herself?"

Tomlinson's pose was still relaxed. But there was something about the way he asked his question. Her uneasiness intensified.

"Dark hair, heavy makeup. Pretty tough."

"Dark hair, huh?"

"With purple streaks."

"How about ten years ago?"

Okay, she was busted. And she was pretty sure she knew who had ratted her out. "Blond."

"Like you?"

"Like me." She gave him a tense smile.

He didn't return it. "Why didn't you tell me you were related to one of the victims?"

"I was afraid you would take me off the case."

"You lied to me, Lexi."

"No, I didn't lie. I told you I knew Kayla."

"You withheld important information."

Her eyes drifted to her lap and she took a stabilizing breath, trying to gather her wits. If she didn't do some fast talking, he was going to assign someone else to lead the investigation.

She brought her gaze back to his and kept it there, unwavering. "Sir, I'm sorry I wasn't completely honest with you. But I was afraid you would make me step down. And this case is important to me. It was before Kayla was killed. And it's even more so now. We're making headway. Please let me continue. Please don't take this away from me."

Tomlinson stared at her, his dark eyes unreadable. If the sternness had lessened, it wasn't by much.

Finally he sighed. "Lexi, you're one of my best detectives. But you're too close to this. It's way too personal for you."

"But that isn't affecting my performance. Look how far I've gotten."

"But your relationship to Kayla could make you take bold risks. Unnecessary risks that you wouldn't take if it was just another murder investigation."

"I won't. I'm careful. I know I can't do Kayla or the other victims any good if I'm dead."

"You look like Lysandra, the next one on the killer's list, which makes you a shoo-in to be his next victim."

Tomlinson was coming up with one reason after another. No problem. She would refute each argument as soon as it left his mouth.

"I can be bait. Better me than some naive young

girl. I'm trained. This might be our best chance of catching this guy."

"It's not safe. I'm not putting you in known danger. He's already threatened you."

"We don't know that for sure. It could have been a prank. Anybody could have written it."

"Sorry, Lexi. I'm assigning Detective Kaminski to take over the case. It's for your good and the good of the case."

She heaved a sigh and her shoulders sagged. So she was well respected. A lot of good it was doing her now. "Sarge, please."

He held up a hand, signaling the end of the discussion, and rose from the chair. "I want you to go over everything with him and bring him up to speed on these latest developments."

She walked from his office, disappointment heavy in her chest. There was no changing his mind. Thanks to Alan, she was off the case. He had betrayed her.

She returned to her cubicle, gathered up her papers and threw her purse over her shoulder. It was lunchtime. Usually she would grab something from the Publix deli right up the road. But now she wanted to be alone.

What had she been thinking? How could she have even considered a future with Alan? She was better off alone.

She slid into the Mazda and tossed her purse and file into the passenger's seat. When she pulled into her driveway fifteen minutes later, her mood wasn't any better than it had been when she left the station. And it probably wouldn't improve until she had the opportunity to unload on Alan.

She wasn't going to let him off the hook on this for a long time, if ever. Getting close to him had somehow made him think he had the right to interfere in her life. She wouldn't excuse herself from the case, so he'd gone behind her back and had her removed. He was treating her just as her mother always had.

Well, she wasn't going to put up with it. After twenty years of living under her mother's controlling, manipulative thumb, she had won her independence. She wasn't about to trade it for the male version of what she had endured for most of her life.

She unlocked and pushed open the front door. As always, Suki met her in the foyer. If she took a sandwich into the living room and plopped down in front of the TV, she would probably have all three cats nestled in around her. The idea had appeal. An hour of Court TV, listening to someone else's problems instead of thinking about her own, and she would be ready to face the rest of her day.

This afternoon she would brief Detective Kaminski. It wouldn't take much. He had helped investigate the first four murders and had been initially involved in this one. So he was already well acquainted with the case.

This evening she would see if her mother needed anything. She had already confronted her about her lies. And she had been all profuse apology. But Lexi knew her mother's brand of apology. She wasn't sorry for her actions. She was just sorry she had been caught.

Then there would be one more Harmony Grove stop to make. Alan would probably be watching for her. He couldn't really expect her to accept his betrayal and go on as if nothing had happened. He had to know her better than that.

At least she'd realized her mistake before she'd gotten in too deep. There was no ring, no seriously hurt feelings on either end. They could both easily jump back to where they were a month ago—two professionals temporarily working together.

She slathered some mayonnaise on two slices of bread and piled on the cheese and lunch meat. Within moments of settling onto the couch she had company. Times three.

Alan had done her a favor. She was happy alone, and she really didn't want to upset her routine. She had been on her own too long, just her and her cats. And it was better that way. She was happy with her life.

But that didn't make Alan's actions hurt any less.

Alan drove slowly down Main Street, window down and arm resting in the opening. The sun sat low on the horizon, staining the western sky vibrant shades of orange, pink and lavender. Another sunny spring day coming to a close, another uneventful shift ended.

As he rolled past Pappy's Pizzeria on his way to the station, enticing aromas drifted to him on the early-evening breeze. His stomach rumbled an impatient response. It was tempting. But Pappy's was better shared. Tonight it would be iced tea and a frozen dinner for one in the company of evening sitcoms.

He cast a glance to his left where a huge oak occupied the vacant space between Dani's Bakery and Westbrook Insurance Agency. Two sets of legs dangled from one of the lower branches.

He frowned. Dani's had closed an hour ago, Westbrook two. No one had any legitimate reason to be hanging around either business. Probably a couple of kids up to no good.

He eased to a stop in one of the parallel parking spaces. As he stepped from the car, the legs disappeared. Yep, definitely up to no good.

And he was reasonably sure he could identify one of the culprits. Whenever there was any kind of shenanigans going on, Duncan Alcott was usually at the center of the mess.

By the time he had reached the other side of the street, sounds came from the tree—a whisper, followed by a harsh "Shh." Whoever they were, they weren't being very stealthy.

He crossed the sparse lawn and stopped at the base of the tree. Two sets of eyes looked down at him. He zeroed in on the instigator, who had apparently tried unsuccessfully to hide a crinkled paper bag in a crook of the branch above him.

"Whatcha got there, Duncan?"

"Nothing."

"Doesn't look like nothing to me. You wanna toss it down here? Otherwise I'll have to climb up there and get it, and that won't make me very happy. You don't wanna see me unhappy, do you?"

Duncan shook his head and reached for the bag. Alan waited. A moment later it dropped into his hands with a thunk and a muffled slosh. He didn't have to look into the bag to know that he wasn't holding Kool-Aid or Pepsi.

"Where'd you get this?"

"It's my dad's."

"Correction. It *was* your dad's." He unscrewed the lid and began to pour out the pungent substance.

"Aw, man. My dad's going to be ticked that you dumped out his booze."

"Your dad needs to keep his booze out of the hands of minors."

He shifted his attention to the other occupant of the tree, this one female.

"You don't look twenty-one, either."

"No, sir, I'm sixteen."

"So you're too young for this stuff, too."

She shook her head, eyes wide. "Oh, no, sir, I don't drink."

Right. No one ever admitted guilt, even when caught red-handed. Except for some reason, Alan was inclined to believe her. Maybe it was that clean, wholesome girl-next-door look. Maybe it was the sincerity and innocence in her eyes. That wasn't likely to last long, hanging with Duncan Alcott.

Which was a shame. She seemed like a nice girl. With blond hair and wispy features, she sort of reminded him of Lexi at that age. He had seen her before, but he didn't know her name. She and her family had moved to Harmony Grove about a month ago. And the past two Sundays they had occupied a pew not far from the front at Cornerstone Community Church.

"Do your parents know where you are?"

"Yes, sir. Well, no, not exactly. But they know that I went for a walk with Duncan. They just said I had to be back before dark."

Alan cast a glance upward, where the sky was rapidly deepening to navy. "Then you'd better get moving."

"Yes, sir. That's what I told Duncan right before you drove up." She scrambled down out of the tree, Duncan right on her heels.

He watched them scurry toward the sidewalk, then called out, "Young lady?"

She turned, brows raised. "Yes, sir?"

"Be careful how you choose your friends."

"Yes, sir."

Something in her smile told him she knew exactly what she was doing. Maybe she was going to have a good influence on Duncan rather than the other way around. He hoped so. The kid needed some positive examples in his life.

He climbed into the cruiser and, two minutes later, swapped it for his Mustang. He had just cranked the engine when his phone began to ring. It was Tomlinson; he recognized the number. He touched the screen and pressed the phone to his ear.

Tomlinson's deep voice came through the phone, crisp and professional. "I'm calling to update you on some changes."

Here we go. "What kind of changes?"

"I've pulled Lexi off the case."

He cringed. "I thought you might."

"I'm putting Detective Sam Kaminski in charge. I want to still keep you in the loop because of your connection with Harmony Grove and the latest victim. Can you write this down?"

"Hold on." He pulled a pen and notepad from the console. "Okay, shoot."

Tomlinson repeated the name and rattled off a phone number. After finishing the call, Alan backed from the parking space. He would program the information into his phone when he got home.

As soon as he turned onto his street, his gut clenched. A blue Mazda sat in his driveway, probably with a very ticked-off Lexi inside. He pulled in next to her and killed the engine. She had swapped cars but hadn't taken the time to change clothes. She was still in uniform.

The stiffness of her shoulders and the set of her jaw announced her displeasure. This wasn't going to be a pleasant exchange.

She exited the vehicle the same time he did and slammed the door a little harder than necessary.

"You ratted on me."

He tried not to flinch under the accusatory glare. "Let's go inside."

She snapped her mouth shut and followed him to the door, staring daggers into his back the whole time. He could feel it.

He unlocked the door and motioned her inside. She spun on him before he even had the door closed.

"I trusted you, and you squealed on me."

He eased the door shut with a soft thud. "I didn't mean for Tomlinson to pull you off the case."

"Oh, yeah? Then what *did* you mean? You called him and volunteered the information that I resemble the young Lysandra, and that Kayla happened to be my cousin. What did you think he was going to do with that? Just ignore it and leave everything be?" Her voice wasn't raised, but the steely edge was unmistakable.

"I told him about Lysandra to ask him to have some units patrol past your house." He stepped toward her and put a hand on her shoulder. "I'm worried about you, Lexi."

"Don't touch me." She jerked away from him and stalked to the other side of the living room. "I can sort of see your reasoning behind asking for units to patrol. It wasn't your place to interfere, but I can understand your point."

She crossed her arms in front of her, further shutting him out. "But I'll never understand why you felt the need to tell him about my relationship with Kayla. The only reason you would have done that was to have me removed from the case."

He strode across the room, but this time had the good sense to stop two feet in front of her. "That wasn't intentional. I was asking for the backup, explaining to him why I was so worried about you. I told him that you weren't going to back down, that you were determined to find your cousin's killer and that I really didn't blame you."

He sighed and looked down at his feet. "I realized I had said too much when Tomlinson asked me if Kayla was your cousin." His gaze again met hers, his own imploring. "I wasn't intentionally telling him something you didn't want him to know. I slipped."

A little bit of the fire seemed to leave her gaze. But she still wasn't happy with him. Not by a long shot.

She stared up at him, arms still crossed. "You put me in a really bad position. Tomlinson feels I lied to him."

"I'm sorry. That wasn't my intent."

"But you still interfered. If everybody would just stay out of my business, my life would be a whole lot less complicated."

She crossed the room with angry strides, brushing past him on her way to the front door. For several moments she stood with her hand resting on the doorknob, as if she wanted to say something but wasn't sure how to say it.

Then she swung open the door and stepped over the threshold. "I'm sick and tired of people trying to control my life." She flung the words over her shoulder just before the door slammed shut.

He moved to the window and separated the slats in the miniblinds in time to see her slide into the driver's seat of the Mazda. She was still miffed. The jerky movements gave it away. So did the clenched jaw and rigid posture.

As she backed from the driveway and sped off down the road, intense emptiness stabbed through him, that void left by thoughts of a future without Lexi.

He was falling for her all over again.

He almost snorted. Who was he kidding? *You can't fall when you never got up to begin with.* All these years he'd never fully recovered from her rejection, never stopped holding out that small sliver of hope that she would one day come back to him. Even while he'd dated his way around town, she had always occupied some almost-forgotten corner of his heart. The casual friendships he'd had with the single women of Harmony Grove had only been cheap substitutes for what he longed for with Lexi.

And now she wanted nothing to do with him. She couldn't even bear his touch.

But there was that one moment of softening, that brief period when his plea seemed to penetrate the thick walls that had gone back up. Maybe she would think about it, realize his good intentions and forgive him for interfering in her life.

Then maybe she would let him make it up to her. Maybe they could start fresh and explore what they'd experienced in the park.

Lord, please make things right between us.

ELEVEN

Lexi put the last of the clean dishes into the cupboard and closed the cabinet doors. Music poured in from the other room, a Mendelssohn piano concerto, backed by a full orchestra.

Her mom's house was always filled with music. If she wasn't producing it herself, a well-planned lineup of her favorite pieces cycled through a top-of-the-line stereo system.

Lexi stepped into the living room where her mom sat in a recliner, an open book in her lap. Although the leg rest was raised as far as it would go, her injured ankle was propped on a thick pillow, elevating it even farther.

Her mom looked up from her reading as soon as Lexi entered the room. "Thank you, dear, for the wonderful dinner and for cleaning everything up."

"No problem. But I need to be heading home. Anything else I can get you before I leave?"

"I can't think of anything." She heaved a forlorn sigh. "I guess if something else comes to mind, I'll just have to figure out how to get it myself."

Lexi squared her shoulders. It was time for the weekly guilt trip, but she wasn't falling for it.

"I think you'll do great. You ought to be an old pro by now getting around with those crutches." She'd had plenty of practice. Not many people could nurse a mild ankle sprain for three and a half weeks.

Her mom chose to ignore the enthusiastic pep talk. She could be as optimistic as the next person. But only when it suited her.

"Sweetheart, I wish you'd consider moving back home, just temporarily. You know, until I can get back on my feet. It's hard to take care of myself. I'm having to hobble here and there on crutches, and I could really use some help."

Lexi gathered her purse and bent to place a kiss on her mother's forehead. For the past four years her mom had dropped hints about her coming back home. But she had gotten really bad in recent weeks. With Lexi's dad gone and Lexi living on her own, her mom had no one left to control. And it was driving her crazy.

"I'll keep coming by and helping you with your laundry and cleaning as long as you need me." She moved toward the door before her mother could say anything else. "Night, Mom."

As she slid into the driver's seat of the Mazda, she shook her head. Her mother needed something to occupy her. A pet or a job or something.

No, not a job. Her mother had never worked a day in her life. She had been pampered by her parents growing up, then pampered by Lexi's dad, to a much lesser degree, all her adult life. And now, thanks to a couple of good insurance policies, she was able to continue her standard of living without having to get a job.

No, what she needed was a pet, some little foo-foo dog that would obey her every whim and gaze at her with undying devotion.

Lexi put the car in Reverse and started to back out of the drive. Four blocks down, a familiar street branched off to the right and tugged at her gaze. Alan's house was almost at the end. He was probably inside, stretched out with a book or chilling in front of the TV. Or maybe he was out on one of his dates. At least if he was with someone else, he wouldn't be meddling in *her* life.

She turned onto Highway 17 and pressed the pedal to the floor, watching the RPMs spike before backing off to shift to the next gear. There were times when she was thankful that she had moved away from Harmony Grove, and this was one of them. Being able to put distance between herself and Alan was a good thing. And now that she had been taken off the case, it would be even easier.

His good looks and sweet ways had almost sucked her in. Spending so much time together, working toward a common goal and bound by their love for Kayla, the whole experience had wreaked havoc with her defenses. Sunday's picnic in the park and romantic walk around the lake had almost finished her off.

But that hadn't lasted long. It had taken all of two days for her to remember why she valued her independence. Being pulled from the case was the pits, but Alan had done her a favor. He truly had.

She eased off the gas at a reduced-speed-ahead sign and frowned. She had accused Alan of being like her mother. But after years of fighting to hold on to every piece of herself she could, maybe she was a little hypersensitive. Because the more she thought about it, the more she had to admit that everything Alan had done came from concern for her rather than his own selfish desires. That alone made him totally different from her mother.

At some point she needed to talk to him. She couldn't stay mad forever. But when that time came, she was going to take it slow.

A ringtone cut into her thoughts, and she pulled off the road to dig for her phone. The number on the screen wasn't familiar, and uneasiness trickled over her, leaving goose bumps in its wake. Would she ever be able to look at a strange number on her phone without fear slashing through her?

Heart thumping, she put the phone to her ear.

"Is this Lexi? This is Jennifer Rushdan. I thought it might be you."

"You thought what might be me?"

"Alexis Simmons, the name at the bottom of this flyer."

Lexi sat straighter and squeezed the phone more tightly. "Yeah, that's me."

To all her peers, she had always been simply Lexi. Jen wasn't exactly her peer, but she was the kid sister of one of her peers. She'd grown up two doors down from the Simmons house. And she had somehow gotten hold of one of her and Alan's notices.

"So you have a flyer?"

"I got it from a guy I work with. His younger sister goes to Polk State."

"I see. You don't know someone who has been stopped, do you?"

"Yeah, I got stopped today on my way home from work."

Lexi's heart jumped to double time and a fine sheen of moisture coated her palms. "By someone in an unmarked car?"

"Yep. I think it was a white Toyota Camry. The flashing lights looked like they were coming from his dash. As soon as he stopped me, he turned them off."

That would make sense. He wouldn't want to attract any more attention to himself than necessary. Otherwise, a real officer might stop to offer assistance and instantly recognize him for a fraud.

"So tell me what happened."

"He asked for my license and registration and insurance information. When he looked at my license, he asked if that was the correct address. I told him it was. He took my stuff back to his car, sat in there for a couple of minutes, then brought everything back to me."

"Did he say why he stopped you?"

"Yeah, he said I was speeding. I was, too. But he didn't give me a ticket. Just told me to slow down."

"What did he look like?"

"He was in a dark green uniform."

"You're sure?"

"Positive. But you know how they normally have patches on the sleeves and a nameplate over the shirt pocket? Well, his didn't have any. It was just a plain dark green uniform. But there was a silver star over the pocket. It said Sheriff, but that's all."

Definitely not a real sheriff's deputy. But close enough to fool someone not paying attention. Or not warned.

"What else can you tell me about him?"

"He had, like, a buzz cut. His hair was a brownish color."

"How about height and weight?"

"I never got out of the car, so I don't know about his height. But he was average weight. Pretty muscular."

"Age?"

"Maybe thirty."

"Any tattoos, distinguishing characteristics, jewelry?"

"No, none of that. I was paying attention, too, because Darrel just gave me the flyer yesterday."

"Okay, you did good, Jen."

"So what now?"

"We'll get some officers to stake out your house. They'll be there every night until he comes back."

There was a long pause, as if Jen had just now considered the possibility that he might come back for her. "Lexi? Will you stay with me?" Her voice had suddenly grown thin and weak.

"How about staying with your parents tonight? Then from tomorrow night on, the detectives will be there. They'll be right outside. So you'll be safe."

"I don't want to be alone. I'm scared. Please?"

"All right. I'll stay." Tomlinson probably wouldn't be happy. But Jen was bait. If she wanted company, she would have it.

As soon as she disconnected the call, Lexi dialed Tomlinson.

"You know those flyers that Alan and I passed out? If you remember, it's my number that's at the bottom. Well, we got a bite."

"Tell me about it."

"She's twenty-five, finished school three years ago. But a coworker of hers got a flyer from his younger sister who's a student at Polk State. She said the uniform was dark green, like ours, but she didn't see the sheriff's department patch on the sleeve. I'm going to check to see if anything was actually run."

"*You're* not doing anything." Tomlinson's voice was low but held a steely edge. "Give the girl's info to Kaminski."

Lexi sighed. "Come on, Sarge. I'm perfectly safe stuck behind a computer." She tried to keep the resentment out of her tone, but wasn't quite successful.

"I'm not backing down on this, Lexi. This isn't your case anymore. It's Kaminski's. Get the girl's info to him, and we'll stake out her place. I assume she lives alone?"

Lexi let her head fall back against the seat, her shoulders slumping in resignation. "Yeah. I've known her all her life. She grew up a couple doors down from me. But she's been on her own for the past three years."

"Another Harmony Grove resident. I'll tell Kaminski to include Alan on this."

Oh, yeah, rub it in. Alan would be hiding out, ready to spring, while she sat tucked away in the house, safe from harm.

"She asked me to stay with her."

"No."

"She begged me. I promised her I would."

"I don't want you anywhere near there. I don't trust you to not jump in and get involved."

"Come on, Sarge. She's scared to death. Let me stay with her."

Silence stretched through the line while he thought. Finally he sighed. "Okay, Simmons. I'll allow it this time. But you stay inside with the girl. I don't want to hear of you taking any unnecessary chances."

"Yes, sir."

She would do as Tomlinson said. She would stay inside.

But if it came down to watching Jen being drugged with chloroform, ready to be dragged away and murdered, no way was she going to stand idly by, hoping that backup was just outside.

She would take the creep down.

* * *

Alan tried to wipe the rain from his eyes with the sleeve of his shirt. It didn't help. There wasn't a square inch of dry cloth anywhere on his body. Although the rain had slowed to a light drizzle, he was cold, wet and miserable.

For the past two hours he had huddled under the overhang while wind gusts drove icy droplets into his face. Detectives Kaminski and Ford were also there, Ford on the opposite side of the house and Kaminski behind the hedge that ran the length of the front, broken by the porch.

And Lexi was inside. Dry and comfortable. The same place she had been for the past two nights. She was probably still mad at him. At least he assumed so. He hadn't actually talked to her. She had seemed bent on avoiding him all week.

He pushed himself away from the wall and walked out into the yard. The worst of the rain had passed, but heavy clouds obscured the night sky. A brilliant half-moon was up there somewhere. He had seen it the past two nights.

On those nights, Lexi had been inside, likely seething, furious at him for his part in having her removed from the case. Tonight she was probably gloating, figuring a little bit of discomfort served him right.

He pulled his soggy shirt away from his chest where it had molded itself. What he wouldn't give for a hot shower. Some dry clothes wouldn't be bad, either. It was going to be a long night.

A long, *unproductive* night, if it was anything like the previous two.

The killer showing up tonight was a long shot. If he didn't come out when the skies were clear and the air a balmy seventy degrees, he wasn't likely to show up on a miserable night like this. Which meant they would be right back out here tomorrow night. And the night after that and the night after that. They finally had a chance of catching this guy. They knew the "where." And the "who" was Jen. But the "when" was anybody's guess.

With a sigh, he headed toward an oak tree that shaded a good portion of the front yard. That had been his hiding place before the downpour had chased him up against the house. The tree trunk was large enough to hide behind but offered him a clear view of Jen's front yard and the back and one side of the Carson place. The two houses shared a drive. It branched off toward the Carsons' garage, then continued all the way back to Jen's cottage.

Alan crossed his arms and leaned back against the trunk of the tree. The boredom was getting to him as much as the soggy clothes. Tomorrow he would consider downloading some MP3s. Good music and interesting podcasts would go a long way toward getting him through the night.

He sighed again, letting his gaze travel to the end of the street. A car turned onto Oakwood Lane and anticipation coursed through him. A dead-end road,

Oakwood hadn't seen much activity since dark. None in the past hour.

The car came closer, passing under a streetlight. Definitely a Toyota Camry. The same Camry that had stopped Jen? They would find out momentarily.

Suddenly, the headlights went out.

Alan tensed, heart pounding in his chest. There was only one reason to cruise down the street with lights off. To avoid being seen. Even if the Camry driver wasn't the killer, he was up to no good.

The car continued to move at a crawl, barely visible in the distant glow of the streetlight. It passed in front of the Carson house, then disappeared from view. Alan held his breath and waited. Moments later, it reappeared and came to a slow stop at the end of the driveway. After several tense moments, the wheels turned hard to the right, and it resumed its forward movement, tires crunching against gravel as it rolled into the drive.

Yes! The killer was falling for their trap. If all went as planned, once Jen opened the door and he pulled out his chloroform-soaked cloth, they would storm the house and capture him. In a few minutes it would all be over. Six months of hard work brought to a satisfying close.

But instead of continuing up the drive, the Camry stopped. The wheels turned again, this time to the left, and the car began to back toward the Carsons' garage. What was he doing?

The next moment, realization extinguished his

excitement. *No, not there!* Number 410 was all the way to the back, 408 at the front. *Come on, it's marked.* Right at the beginning of the drive.

Alan watched from fifty feet away, praying the killer would figure it out. Finally the driver's door swung open. But the dome light didn't come on. He had turned it off. The guy was careful. Of course, they already knew that.

For several moments he stood next to the car, door open. He seemed to be scanning the area, looking for danger, ears cocked for the slightest movement.

Alan longed to move closer, maybe even try to get a tag number. But he didn't dare. The guy was on edge, superalert. It was obvious in the way he stood, the tension that emanated from him. Nothing would escape his notice. A rustle of clothing, the snap of a twig, and he would take off.

Finally he moved away from the car and began to walk toward the house. The *wrong* house. The Carsons were home, and though it was almost eleven o'clock, they hadn't gone to bed. Several lights were on inside, and a television filled one room with a soft, bluish glow.

The suspect stepped from view, presumably headed to the front door. Alan cast a glance at Kaminski, who was watching from around the corner of Jen's house. After a nod and gesture from the older detective, Alan sprang from his hiding place to sprint toward the Carson house. Plans had just changed.

He stayed in the shadows as much as possible,

moving from tree to tree and finally ducking behind one of the shrubs that sparsely lined the opposite side of the drive. He had just straightened to dive behind the next one when the driver reappeared, hurrying toward his car.

Alan crouched behind the shrub and waited. Maybe the suspect realized he had the wrong house and would just continue up the drive. When he did, Kaminski and Ford would be waiting for him.

But instead of driving into the trap set for him, he took off in a spray of gravel and slid sideways several inches before hitting the road. Alan grabbed his radio and shot across the Carsons' yard. Just as he reached the road, the car sped past, lights still off. By the time he had radioed in the description, both Kaminski and Ford stood next to him.

Kaminski, the older one, was breathing harder than Ford. "Did you get a good look at him?"

Alan shook his head. "It was too dark, and I wasn't able to get close enough."

"Tag number?"

"I couldn't get that, either. He kept his lights off all the way to the end of the street. By the time he passed under the streetlight, he was too far away."

"Which way did he turn?"

"Right." Away from Harmony Grove, which wasn't any surprise.

"He may suspect we're on to him."

Kaminski took a diagonal path to the drive through Carsons' front yard. Alan followed, and Ford fell in beside him. When they reached the corner of the garage, the front door of the house swung open and Willie Carson stepped onto the porch. He was barefoot, dressed in plaid cotton pajamas that were a little too short for his tall, lanky frame.

Alan backtracked to meet him. He had given the Carsons sketchy information earlier in the week, letting them know they would be there. But this was the first night Willie had ventured outside.

"Did you see something?"

Willie nodded. "Sure did. The missus and me was gettin' ready for bed, and I was turnin' off lights. When I walked into the livin' room, someone was at the window. He saw me and took off."

"Can you describe him for me?"

"'Fraid not. Couldn't see him that good through the screen, light being on inside and all."

"If you think of anything else that might help us, give me a call."

"Sure will." Willie's head bobbed. "Anything I can do to help. If he comes back, I'll get my .22."

Alan held up a hand. "Let's not get carried away. Just call me. No shooting anybody."

Willie nodded again, his enthusiasm a little more restrained. He had worked in one of the phosphate mines all his life and recently retired. This was probably the most excitement he'd had in a while.

When Alan rejoined the others, they had all gathered in the cottage at the back. Jen and Lexi sat at the kitchen table nursing what looked like two glasses of iced tea. Ford stood behind a third chair, and Kaminski leaned against the doorjamb, pose casual.

Kaminski raised a brow at him. "Well?"

"I know why the suspect ran. Willie Carson went to turn off the living room light and came face-to-face with him."

"What do you think the chances are that he'll be back?"

Alan thought for a moment. "Probably not good. If he thinks Jen lives in the house at the front, he believes she's not alone. And he only targets women who are alone."

His gaze drifted to Lexi, and she lifted her chin. She didn't need the reminder. But he would give it anyway. Every chance he got.

"And," he continued, "if he realized his mistake and knows Jen lives in the cottage at the back, he still probably won't be back. He knows we're watching her place."

Alan's running to the road had guaranteed that. But getting a tag number had been their best chance at identifying him. And he couldn't pass it up.

Kaminski pushed himself away from the wall. "Well, I think we're through here tonight. What do you say we all go home and get into some dry clothes?"

Alan smiled. "You won't get any argument from me."

Ford and Kaminski moved toward the front door, but Alan hung back. Creases of concern had settled into Jen's face as she watched the two detectives leave. His reasoning about the killer not returning apparently hadn't done much to allay her fears.

His gaze locked with Lexi's. "You staying?"

"I will for tonight."

Tension seemed to drain suddenly from Jen, and her breath escaped in a relieved sigh. "Thanks. I think I'll go stay with Mom and Dad for a while until this is all over." She directed a weak smile Alan's way. "Just in case."

"That's a good idea." He returned her smile, then moved toward the door. "I guess I'll leave you ladies alone."

Once outside, he headed up the gravel drive and to the house just past the Carsons'. He had left his Mustang there. Kaminski and Ford had ridden together in Kaminski's 4Runner, which they had parked across the street. It, of course, was gone. Lexi's car was in the Carsons' garage. At least, that was what he had been told. He hadn't personally seen it. She had always managed to get there a little ahead of him.

He had hoped for a chance to talk to her. It hadn't come. Three straight nights and he hadn't had two seconds alone with her. Maybe he should just show up at her house. With flowers. And a sincere apology.

He slid into the driver's seat of his Mustang and shut the door.

Yep, a bouquet of flowers was a good idea.

TWELVE

"Simmons, meet me in my office."

Tomlinson caught her before she even made it to her cubicle. He walked at a good clip, holding a file folder, Greg Morganson a pace or two behind. Lexi changed direction and followed. At least this time she wouldn't be getting a dressing-down, not with Greg present to witness it.

When he reached his office, instead of rounding the desk to sit behind it, Tomlinson leaned against the front, propping a hip on top. "We had a call from a waitress at a local wings place. Seems one of her frequent customers wasn't getting enough of her with his wings and beer. He started hounding her outside of work. He never tried to talk to her, just kept show-ing up where she was. Even joined the same gym so he could watch her work out."

"Perv." Lexi muttered the word under her breath, but Tomlinson heard, if the quirk of his lips was any indication.

"It was bad enough that she got a restraining order.

But that didn't stop him. This morning we found him parked across the street from her apartment complex, a pair of binoculars in front of his face and a camera with a monster zoom lens sitting next to him."

"So he's been taken into custody?"

Tomlinson nodded.

"Good." The creep would probably say she brought it on herself with the short shorts and eye-popping cleavage. But nothing excused what he did.

"Anyway," Tomlinson continued, "we've put in for a warrant and should have it anytime now. I want you two to search his place and see what you can find."

Lexi nodded. She was a homicide detective. Chasing stalkers was a far cry from solving murders. But this was how a lot of killers started—obsessed and perverted. Maybe she could take this one off the street before some innocent girl lost her life.

"What can you tell us about the suspect?"

"The guy's name is Wendell Moorehead. White male, forty-three, five foot eleven, a hundred eighty pounds. He works part-time for one of the aluminum contractors, keeping the shop cleaned up. Lives in a two-bedroom house on the edge of Lakeland. Apparently has a roommate."

She glanced over at Greg. He hadn't spoken but was busy taking notes. She frowned. Not only had Tomlinson pulled her from Kayla's case, he was giving her a newbie detective to babysit. Nothing against Greg. He seemed nice enough. But she wasn't a trainer. She got too wrapped up in her own investigating to take the time to teach someone else.

Tomlinson moved away from the desk and headed for the door. "Go on over there. I'll call you as soon as we have the warrant."

Lexi walked with Greg through the station and out to the parking lot.

"I'll drive." Her tone didn't leave him any room to argue.

He buckled himself into the passenger seat and waited until she had left the parking lot to strike up conversation.

"How long have you been with the department?"

"Four years."

"Like it?"

"Oh, yeah. It's challenging." She glanced over at him. "How about you?"

"Yeah, I like it. But you've got a lot of time on me. I've got seven months to your four years."

She nodded and reached for the radio dial. Soft rock filled the confines of the car.

"Are you single?"

What is this, Twenty Questions? She never cared for that game. And "Let's Get to Know Our Coworkers" wasn't much better.

"Single and not looking to change that status anytime soon." She cringed at the snarky tone that came through in her voice. He was just being friendly. It wasn't his fault that Alan had gotten her pulled off Kayla's case. "How about you?"

"Yeah, I'm single. The old lady dumped me and ran off with my best friend."

She frowned. That was more than she needed to know. "Sorry to hear that."

"Don't be. I say 'good riddance.' Now it's just me and my dog." Greg settled back in the seat and looked straight ahead. "Anyway, that's when I decided to get into police work. You know, make a new start. That was three years ago."

"What kind of dog do you have?"

"A black Lab. I rescued him from the pound, so he thinks the sun rises and sets on me. And I think *he's* pretty cool, too. Much less demanding than a woman." He smiled over at her. "No offense."

By the time she stopped in front of the Lakeland address Tomlinson had given her, he had called with news of the warrant, and she had heard half of Greg's life story. At least his adult life.

She walked to the front door and rang the bell. There were no vehicles in the drive. The roommate was probably at work. But kicking in doors was a last resort.

A quick survey of the property, however, left them no choice. The front and side doors were locked, with no keys hidden outside, and the dog that guarded the back appeared none too happy about two uniformed strangers roaming his yard.

She left the dog barking and growling inside the back fence and walked to the side door. Before she could kick it in, Greg stopped her.

"Here, let me."

Whatever. She didn't have anything to prove. She stepped back and moments later the door swung open, exposing a splintered jamb.

A hallway led them past a small laundry area and into the kitchen. Her gaze scanned the room. Definitely the residence of a couple of stereotypical bachelors. Dirty dishes filled the sinks and sat on the countertop in haphazard stacks. The dishwasher was open, its racks almost empty. From the looks of things, they were one meal away from dirtying their last clean dish.

Greg walked into what appeared to be a living room, and she followed a short hall that led from the kitchen to a bedroom. An open pizza box sat on a computer desk, one piece of dried-up pizza still inside. Clothes overflowed a hamper in the corner, and the bed was unmade, the sheets wrapped around the comforter in a jumbled mess. As she stepped farther into the room, Greg's voice stopped her.

"Lexi, you'd better come and look at this."

She hurried toward the other end of the house. Off the living room was a second bedroom. Greg stood looking at a corkboard mounted over a desk. There were two others just like it, all covered in photos. A couple of expensive-looking lenses sat on the desk. The camera and at least one lens would have been taken into evidence when the suspect was arrested.

She approached one of the boards. The photos all seemed to be of the same woman. Shoulder-length dark hair, young, attractive and well endowed. Judging from the attire in some of the pictures, this was the wings waitress.

Greg moved to stand beside her. "She looks like a tease."

Something in his tone set her off, a touch of judgment. "Are you insinuating that she deserved this unwanted attention?" Her voice held a testy edge.

He raised both hands. "Not at all. Just making an observation."

She moved to the next board. This subject was blond, equally attractive. In some of the pictures she wore a medical uniform.

"The guy was stalking the nurse at his doctor's office?"

Lexi frowned. "That's what it looks like."

The last board held photos of yet another subject. This one appeared to be Asian. None of the pictures revealed what she did for a living. They were all candid shots—shopping, standing on a sidewalk, getting into her car, hanging with friends. Lexi leaned forward. With those exotic features and jet-black hair, she was gorgeous.

Greg let out a low whistle. "How much you wanna bet none of these women had any idea they were being photographed?"

"No doubt. He was probably fifty feet away, shooting them with a zoom lens."

Her gaze circled the room, then came to rest on a bookcase in the corner. The entire top shelf looked like it was packed full of photo albums. She pulled one from the center.

"People don't usually have this many photo albums. Proud parents, yes. A single guy living with his roommate? Not likely."

She flipped through the pages. Just as she expected. More pictures like those on the boards—candid shots of beautiful women, probably all shot with a zoom lens.

She slid the album back into its slot on the shelf and pulled out another one. It, too, was filled with shots of women. So was the next, and the one after that. Book after book, all the same.

"How long has he been doing this mess?" Greg had stepped up beside her and stood watching her flip the pages.

"Apparently a long time."

She slid the last book onto the shelf and moved toward the closet. The door stood open. It was a walk-in, with racks of clothes on two sides and shoe cubbies built into the back. When she flipped the light switch, nothing happened. Probably a dead bulb.

She stepped inside and scanned the high shelf that ran along all three sides. It held lots of miscellaneous stuff—several shoe boxes, a camera bag, a stack of magazines, some games, a bowl of loose change and…

One object caught her gaze and held it. She stiffened as coldness washed over her and settled in her

core. Sitting on the shelf in plain view was a policeman's hat.

She began pushing hangers down the rod with sharp
flicks of her wrist, her pulse rate picking up speed.
Near the end of the rack, she found it—a policeman's
uniform. There was a patch on the left sleeve: three
V-shaped stripes. A silver star was pinned over the
right pocket, and a pair of handcuffs hung down the
front, looped over the hook of the hanger.

Her heart was pounding in earnest now. Had Tomlinson taken her off Kayla's case, then inadvertently
put her in the killer's house?

"Check this out, Greg." She clicked on her flashlight and shone it on the uniform as he stepped up
beside her.

"A police uniform." His voice was hushed. "The
killer."

"The problem is, it's navy." Even by flashlight in
a darkened closet, she could see the uniform wasn't
dark green.

"Maybe the girl who was abducted was confused.
I mean, she was probably too shaken up to be very
reliable with the details."

"But Jen wasn't shaken up."

"Who's Jen?"

"The girl he stopped last week and pretended to run
her license." Oh, yeah. Greg wouldn't have the latest
details. "Jen paid attention. It was dark, but she got
a pretty good description of the guy. He was average
build, but fairly muscular. And he had a buzz cut."

Greg ran a hand over his closely shaved head and grinned. "That describes a lot of us nowadays."

She returned his smile. "True. But she said the uniform was dark green, and there weren't any patches."

Greg's gaze shifted to the uniform hanging in the closet. "This patch is on the left sleeve. My guess is if we pulled it out of the closet, there wouldn't be anything on the right, and that's the sleeve she would have seen."

Lexi nodded slowly. They wouldn't test his theory, not until after everything was processed. But he had a point. And in the dark, navy blue could possibly be mistaken for dark green.

But there was another inconsistency. "Both witnesses put him around thirty. This guy is forty-three."

"You know how it is when you're young. Thirty, forty, fifty—it's all the same."

No, she didn't know. Even in her teens, someone would have to be a young forty for her to mistake him for thirty. But it was possible. She pulled her phone from the pouch on her belt and dialed Tomlinson.

As soon as he answered, she jumped in. "We'd better get Crime Scene out here. We found pictures. Hundreds of them. And a police uniform."

She filled him in on the rest of the details. When she finished, an unexpected chuckle came through the phone. "I removed you from the case, and it looks like you might have solved it anyway. Good job, Lexi."

"Thanks. By the way, what kind of car was he in when they picked him up this morning?"

"A truck. A Ford F-150."

She frowned, her doubt increasing. "Not a Camry?"

"No, but maybe he has a second vehicle."

"Maybe."

Right after she disconnected the call, the front door creaked open and a hesitant male voice called out.

"Hello?"

She hurried to the front of the house to find a man entering the kitchen. He was a throwback from the sixties era, with blond hair graying at the edges, pulled back into a thin ponytail that almost reached his waist.

He spun to face them. "What's going on? I come home for lunch and there are cops in my house."

Lexi didn't address his question. "What's your name?"

"Jeff Underwood."

"Wendell's your roommate?"

"Yeah."

"How about showing us which room is yours."

He looked from her to Greg and shrugged. "Sure. Right back here."

Lexi followed him down the short hall to the bedroom she had entered on first arriving. "Okay, that's what we needed to know. But you'll have to leave now. We're in the middle of an investigation. Just don't go very far. We'll probably need to talk to you."

"Is Wendell in some kind of trouble?"

"We can't say just yet."

She began walking him toward the front door. He

complied without argument. He was being pretty laid-back about the whole thing.

"What about after work? Can I sleep here tonight?"

"You'd better make other arrangements. We'll let you take some clothes and personal items, but we'll probably be here for the next two days."

Not that she had high hopes of finding anything. It wasn't likely, since none of the victims had been brought there. If the killer was smart and careful enough to strip a whole crime scene of any smidgen of evidence, he wasn't likely to bring anything home with him.

Except pictures. Hundreds of them. The problem was, there wasn't a single photo of any of the five victims.

When they reached the entry area, Jeff gripped the doorknob, then dropped his hand. He turned to face them, brows drawn together. "What did Wendell do?"

"We can't share that yet."

Greg cleared his throat. "Who does the dog in back belong to?"

"He's Wendell's."

"Is someone going to take care of him while Wendell's gone?"

Lexi smiled. They were in the middle of a possible murder investigation, and he was worried about the dog. Nothing wrong with being an animal lover.

"I take care of him any time Wendell goes away." He gripped the knob and swung open the door. "You got a card or something so I can call and find out when I can come back?"

She pulled a business card from her front shirt pocket and handed it to him. Her gaze drifted past him, and her eyes widened.

A Toyota Camry sat in the drive.

It wasn't all the way white. It was two-tone, with that common beige-gold color at the bottom. But the majority of the car was white.

Lexi nodded toward the driveway "Is that yours?"

"The Camry? Yeah. Why?"

"Do you ever loan it to Wendell?"

"Once or twice a long time ago, when his truck was in the shop. Not in the past year. Why?"

"I'm afraid we're going to have to impound it."

"What?" The word exploded from his mouth. He wasn't so laidback anymore. "I need to get back to work."

"Detective Morganson here can take you." She cast a glance at Greg. "Pick him up some lunch, too."

"Come on, man. I'm okay with you taking over my house if Wendell's in some kind of trouble. But what's that got to do with me and my car?"

"If Wendell's gotten into trouble, he's done it in your car."

Jeff shook his head. "No way, man. If he took my car, I would have known it."

She didn't respond, just fished her keys from her pocket and handed them to Greg. They would get the warrant extended to include Jeff's car. If there was evidence to be found, that was where they would find it.

She watched Greg leave, Jeff in the back. The crime scene unit would arrive anytime. Meanwhile, she would see what else she could find.

By the time Greg returned, more than an hour had passed. Crime Scene had already arrived and was processing the bedroom. He held up a bag and cardboard carrier with two drinks, then made his way to the kitchen. An enticing aroma preceded him. She smiled wryly. Her palate must have degraded to basement levels when she classified fast food as enticing. But she was hungry. The drive-through lines must have been long.

Greg pulled out two wrapped sandwiches from the bag and handed her a third. "I got you a grilled chicken. You don't look like a greasy-cheeseburger kind of girl."

Frankly she was a whatever-was-fast kind of girl. But grilled chicken was fine.

After wiping a wet paper towel across the kitchen table, she washed her hands over a mountain of dirty dishes. Greg made the smart decision and washed up in the bathroom instead.

She sank into the chair and unwrapped her sandwich. With the dirty dishes piled up three feet away, it wasn't like eating in her kitchen at home. But she had eaten in worse settings.

Greg took the chair across from her. "Sorry it took me so long to get back here. The drive-throughs were packed, and I had to hit two of them. Jeff wanted Chinese, and I wasn't sure if you did Chinese. So I went for the all American."

She held up her sandwich, now a third of the way eaten. "As you can see, you made a good choice."

"So anything exciting happen while I was gone?"

"Not really. Last I checked, Crime Scene was processing the uniform. Of course, they'll bag it up and take it with them."

"Then what's next? After we're finished here, I mean."

"There's a good chance this will all be turned over to Homicide."

Greg nodded. "That's where I'd like to end up someday. It seems really interesting."

Yeah, that was one way to put it. But she could think of a few other adjectives, too. Such as grueling. And frustrating. And heart wrenching.

"We'll go ahead and get some crime scene tape up. Then I'll get you back to the station." There was no reason for Greg to hang out there the rest of the afternoon while Crime Scene did their tedious work.

Tomorrow she would talk to the suspect. And during the course of the next two days, hopefully they would find the evidence they needed to put this creep away for good.

She stepped out the front door with her heart feeling lighter than it had in months. Tonight she would go see Alan. She was still upset at him for talking to Tomlinson. He'd had no business interfering in her life.

But she was hours away from solving the case.

And for some reason, he was the first one she wanted to tell.

THIRTEEN

Alan pulled into the driveway of the small brick house and disappointment washed over him. The Mazda wasn't there. It was eight o'clock. He had hoped she'd be home by now.

He glanced over at the frosted-glass vase held somewhat secure by the passenger seat belt. Two dozen red roses could atone for a lot of wrongs. At least that was what he was banking on.

He turned off the engine, picked up his phone and brought up Lexi's number. She answered on the third ring. At least she was taking his call. And her "Hello" didn't sound the least bit annoyed. Judging from the background noise, she was driving.

"Where are you?"

"I'm headed to Harmony Grove."

"Going to see your mom?"

"No, you."

A grin climbed up his cheeks. "In that case, turn around. I'm sitting in your driveway."

"What are you doing there?"

"I'm here to see you."

"Dumb question, huh?" There was a smile in her tone. "See you in about ten minutes."

He ended the call, relief coursing through him. This encounter was going to be even more pleasant than he had hoped. Whatever had happened, her anger with him seemed to have evaporated.

True to her word, ten minutes later she rolled to a stop next to him, and by the time she killed the engine and removed her seat belt, he was at her door, roses in hand.

"I come bearing gifts. And words of apology. I'm sorry for going behind your back and talking to Tomlinson. It'll never happen again." He held up a hand. "Scout's honor. Forgive me?"

She climbed from the car and took the roses from him. "The jury's still out on that. But this definitely helps." She flashed him a smile, that same beautiful, sweet smile he had fallen in love with.

He followed her to the door, and she turned to face him on the porch. Excitement shone from her eyes. "I have good news. We might have caught our killer."

His chest tightened, whatever excitement she was projecting tempered by his own fear. "He didn't come back for Jen, did he?"

She unlocked the door and led him inside. "No. We picked him up on a completely unrelated case, stalking. When we checked out his place, we found hundreds of photos."

"What kinds of photos?"

"Women. But none of them were of any of the victims."

"So what makes you think he's the killer?"

She dropped her purse on the coffee table and continued to the kitchen. "After looking at the photos, I checked out his closet. And guess what I found. A police uniform."

She set the vase in the sink and topped off the water before continuing. "It's generic, nothing identifying it as being associated with a particular department. It's navy instead of dark green, but since it was dark when Jen got stopped, she could be mistaken on the color."

"I don't know. She seemed pretty sure." They were going to have to come up with a lot more than that to charge the guy with murder.

"That's what I thought. Then his roommate showed up. In a white Camry." She lifted the vase from the sink and set it on the counter, then flashed him another smile. "Thank you for the roses. I'm keeping them up here so Midnight doesn't eat them. He's usually pretty good about not getting up on the kitchen counter."

He followed her gaze to the flower-eating bandit, who was currently weaving in and out of her legs. So was the vocal Siamese. The big gray one hadn't appeared yet. Lexi picked up Suki and walked into the living room.

As he settled onto the couch next to her, Suki made herself at home on her lap, voicing her contentment with loud purrs.

"Anything else tying him to the killings?"

"We don't have anything back yet from Crime Scene, but I did check out his book-in photo. I know the descriptions we have are pretty vague, but they do fit—buzz cut, muscular. He could possibly even pass for mid-thirties. We're going to do a lineup to see if Jen can identify him. We'll do the same for Denise."

She ran a hand down Suki's back and the cat purred even louder. "The poor girl will finally be able to come home. If she even wants to. The times I've talked to her, she seems pretty content up there. I'm afraid Polk County holds too many bad memories."

He frowned. "It's probably better that she stays put. In case they've got the wrong guy."

"What's wrong?" She cocked a brow at him. "You don't seem convinced."

"You say he's got all these photos of women, right?"

"Hundreds."

"But he apparently didn't kill any of them."

"Not that we know of. We'll be running them through the databases over the next few weeks. Of course, we know one of the women. She filed the restraining order that got him picked up."

"But there isn't a single picture of any of your five victims."

"He's too smart to leave behind that kind of evidence."

He shook his head. "I don't know. You pick the guy

up for stalking, and he just happens to be the killer. It seems too easy. Too coincidental."

She turned to face him more fully and grinned. "Haven't you been praying for divine help?"

"Yeah, but—"

"You don't think your God is big enough to drop the guy in our lap?"

"I have no doubt that God's big enough. I'm just saying that something about this feels off."

She studied him, the smile still there. Finally she gave a short nod. "I've missed you."

"You have?"

"Yep. Our brainstorming sessions, bouncing ideas off each other. We make a good team."

He returned her smile. "We do."

He had missed her, too. And it wasn't just working together on the case. It was everything. Eating together, laughing, talking, walking hand in hand at the park.

And it wasn't just this week. He had missed her for the past six years.

"How about letting me take you out to dinner Friday night?"

As soon as the words were out of his mouth, he wished he could take them back. She hadn't fully forgiven him for talking to Tomlinson. Asking her out was rushing things. "You know," he added, "to discuss the case. Not as a date or anything."

The teasing smile she gave him shattered his reservations.

"But what if I *want* a date with Harmony Grove's most eligible bachelor?"

He matched her smile with one of his own. "Then I'd be happy to oblige."

"I'm looking forward to it."

Her smile faded and her eyes grew warm, emotion flickering in their depths, traces of what used to be there every time she looked at him. Was he really seeing what he thought he saw?

He reached up to run a finger along her jawline. What he wanted to do was to kiss her. But that *would* be rushing things.

"I'm going to leave and let you get some rest." He pushed himself to his feet.

She moved Suki off her lap and let him help her up. "I'm going to question the suspect tomorrow morning. I'll let you know how it goes."

"You want some company?"

"Mmm, probably not. If he feels like we're ganging up on him, he'll be more likely to clam up."

He nodded and moved toward the door. "You might be right. Keep me posted."

"I will. And keep the prayers going, will you?"

"So you're acknowledging that maybe God does listen?"

"I'm leaning a little in that direction." One side of her mouth quirked up. "Who knows? I might even show up at your church one day."

"I'll save you a spot."

A ringtone sounded from her purse on the end table

and she hurried to retrieve her phone. She looked at the screen, then cast him a glance filled with anticipation. "It's Tomlinson."

She pressed the phone to her ear, and moments later, her brows lifted. "That's too much to be mere coincidence. I'm going to the jail tomorrow to interview him. I'll bring that up."

In the next span of silence, her face fell. "Come on, Sarge. I know it's Kaminski's case, but let me do this. If Moorehead's not our killer, this is just a stalking case, and you've already assigned it to me. If he *is* our killer, he's locked up. So I'm safe either way."

Moments later, the corners of her mouth lifted. "Thanks. And no need to call Alan. He's here." Her cheeks flushed a little pink at the admission.

She ended the call and dropped her phone into her purse, eyes shining with excitement. "A bottle was retrieved from under the suspect's bathroom sink."

"What kind of bottle?"

"Brown, made of glass. It has some kind of liquid in it. According to one of the crime scene techs, it's sweet-smelling, made him kind of light-headed."

He raised his brows. "Chloroform?"

"If it's not, I'll eat my socks."

"So how did Tomlinson respond to your argument for letting you interview the suspect?"

She grinned over at him. "He accused me of liking to push the boundaries. But he's letting me do it." She crossed her arms and leaned against the doorjamb. "I know none of the photos Moorehead has are of the dead girls. But what are the chances of him having a police costume, a roommate with a Camry and a bottle of chloroform under the bathroom sink?"

"Pretty slim."

"He *has* to be our guy."

"Unless the chloroform belongs to the roommate. The Camry does."

"But the roommate doesn't fit the description of the killer. Based on the book-in photo, Moorehead does."

Alan nodded and stepped into the balmy evening air.

For her sake, and for the sake of the single young women of Polk County, he hoped she was right.

Lexi sat at the polished oak table, a manila file folder in front of her. It was closed. She didn't need to review what was inside. She had it almost memorized.

But she flipped open the cover anyway and scanned the sheet on top. She may as well, because the room she waited in certainly didn't offer anything of interest. Except for the table, four chairs and a fake plant sitting in the corner, the space was bare. No pictures decorated the plain white walls, just a simple clock—a clock that had advanced fifteen minutes since she'd entered the room.

She dropped her gaze back to her folder until the rattle of the doorknob caught her attention. The door swung open and a corrections officer led in an inmate in an orange jail jumpsuit.

"This is Moorehead." The officer turned toward the door. "I'll be waiting outside."

She watched him leave the room, then nodded toward the chair opposite her. "Have a seat, Wendell. It's all right if I call you Wendell?"

"Sure. Whatever."

He settled into the chair and leaned back, weight shifted to one side in a devil-may-care pose that he didn't quite pull off.

"I'm Alexis Simmons. I have a few questions for you. I spent a good bit of yesterday at your house."

A flicker of concern flashed across his features— so brief she might have imagined it.

"It seems you have a pretty impressive collection of photos."

"I'm a hobby photographer. There's nothing illegal about that."

"There is when you're doing it thirty feet from a woman who has a restraining order against you."

He shrugged and one side of his mouth cocked up in an irreverent half grin. "I've been through this before. They're not going to keep me that long."

"You might be a guest of Polk County longer than you think. So tell me, what's the police uniform for?"

"What's that got to do with anything?"

"Just answer the question."

"It's a costume."

"What for?"

"My company's harvest party. We do it every year,

the last weekend in October. It's a costume party. I've gone as a cop the past three years."

"What company is this?"

"Davis Aluminum."

That would be easy enough to check out. They were a good-size aluminum contractor, right on one of the main drags through Lakeland.

"How long have you worked there?"

"About four years."

She nodded. That cocky air was as pronounced as ever, but at least he was answering her questions.

"What's in the brown bottle under your bathroom sink?"

"What brown bottle? You're going to have to be more specific."

"A brown bottle about five inches tall, glass, unmarked."

"How am I supposed to know? I'm sure there are all kinds of bottles under there."

"They tell me it smells an awful lot like chloroform."

He gave an irreverent smirk. "I don't know what you're talking about."

"Chloroform. Puts people out. Women are a lot more cooperative when they're unconscious. Not nearly as feisty."

He stiffened and sat straighter. That cockiness was falling away by the second, and concern was moving in. "What are you trying to pin on me?"

"I'm not trying to pin anything on you. I'm just trying to get at the truth."

"Well, you've already got the truth. I went out and took some pictures. That's the extent of it." He once again settled back into that nonchalant pose, but now that cockiness held an undercurrent of fear.

"When is the last time you drove the Camry?"

"What Camry?"

"Jeff's Camry."

"I don't drive Jeff's car. I've got my own."

"How about after he goes to bed at night?"

"Why would I do that?"

"I don't know. Maybe you don't want to be seen driving your own car?"

"What, has some kind of a crime been committed using a white Camry?" He gave a snicker. "Someone going around stealing doughnuts? Got you cops in an uproar?"

"Maybe. But we're more concerned about the girls who are being murdered."

His eyes widened and he raised both hands. "Hey, lady, that's not me. Okay, I admit it. I like women. I like to look at them and admire them and photograph them. But I'd never raise a hand to hurt one of them. If you're looking for a killer, you got the wrong guy."

The last trace of cockiness had dissolved with the word *murdered*. Nervousness had replaced the smooth, confident air. A telltale tightness stiffened his jaw, and one leg bounced a rapid rhythm. She couldn't see under the table, but she didn't need to. The movement radiated all the way into his torso.

"You don't have anything on me."

"We'll see. My buddies are working hard at your place. And you'd better believe we're going to be thoroughly checking out that uniform of yours. It's amazing the stories that the tiniest of particles can tell. A strand of hair, a clothing fiber. And of course, we've taken in the Camry."

His eyes widened again. "You impounded Jeff's car? He's gonna kill me."

"He'll get it back when we're done."

He lifted his chin and cast her a disdainful glance. "You guys are grasping at straws. Do you know how many white Camrys there are on the roads?"

"A lot. But most other Camry drivers don't happen to have a police uniform hanging in their closet and a bottle of chloroform under their sink. So that makes you a pretty good suspect."

"Well, I'm not a Camry driver, and I don't know anything about any chloroform. So looks like you're batting one out of three. Not very good odds, I'd say."

Lexi pulled a photo from the folder and laid it in front of him. It was an earlier picture of the first victim. She was gagged and restrained, but not too badly beaten yet. "Do you know this lady?"

As soon as his gaze fell on the picture, he turned away and pushed it back across the table. "I'm not saying anything else without a lawyer."

"No problem." She stood and crossed the room.

After she knocked twice, the door swung open. "We're finished here."

She walked from the room, leaving Wendell Moorehead in the hands of the officer. Moorehead was a jerk and a creep and a pervert. But was he a killer? Something in her gut told her no. She needed to go back to the station and talk to Tomlinson. And tonight she would run everything by Alan.

Maybe she would talk to Alan sooner.

She slid into the seat and plucked her phone from her side. When he answered, an involuntary smile crept up her cheeks. "What are you doing?"

"Working."

"Are you available for an interview this afternoon?"

"For you, I'm always available."

Warmth infused her chest and a pleasant tingle swept over her. "Can you meet me at one? Davis Aluminum, 98 North. You familiar with it?"

"I'll be there with bells on."

"That's a scary picture."

When she walked into the station, she met Greg Morganson heading out. She nodded a greeting and he turned to follow her.

"Sarge says you're going to interview the suspect."

"Just coming from there."

She kept walking and he fell in beside her.

"Learn anything interesting?"

"Yeah. He says he got the cop costume to wear to

his company harvest party. Says he's worn it for the past three years."

"What did he have to say about the Camry and the chloroform?"

"He doesn't know anything about the chloroform and never drives his roommate's car."

"You don't believe him, do you?"

She looked over at him and shrugged. "I haven't decided yet."

"How likely do you think it is that someone can have chloroform under their bathroom sink and not know it's there?"

"It depends on how observant they are."

"If a strange brown bottle showed up under *my* sink, *I* would notice. If you ask me, he's guilty as sin. Chloroform is a controlled substance, not a common item in the average guy's house. Between that, the uniform and the Camry, it's too much to be mere coincidence."

"Maybe." But something didn't sit right with her. Greg was a newbie; he would go with the most obvious explanation.

She stopped outside Tomlinson's open doorway. "A lot of solving crimes is going with your gut. And my gut tells me we've got the wrong guy."

When she entered Tomlinson's office, he was watching her with a knowing smile.

"Have a seat. You, too, Greg. Tell me how it went."

She sank into the padded chair, and Greg settled in next to her.

"As you probably gathered, I met with Wendell Moorehead. He's cocky, irreverent and a perv. Definitely rubs me the wrong way. But I don't think he's our killer."

Tomlinson nodded slowly and turned his attention to Morganson. "What do you think, Greg? You spent several hours at the suspect's house. What's your take on all this?"

Greg seemed to sit a little straighter. Tomlinson was good at building morale in those under his supervision, making them feel valued and competent.

"I think we've got him. The police uniform and the fact that his roommate has a Camry, those two things raised my suspicions. But finding the chloroform under the sink clinched it for me."

"That's a good point."

Lexi shook her head. "Stalking women to collect their photos doesn't fit with what we know of the killer. He's out for vengeance, every murder a payback for wrongs done ten years earlier."

"One doesn't rule out the other," Greg argued. "Just because he likes to stalk women and take their pictures doesn't negate the possibility that he's also on a vendetta. I'm sure we've got our guy. I just hope we can get enough on him to bring him to justice."

Tomlinson stayed silent while they debated back and forth. Greg was as sure of his position as Lexi was of hers.

Lexi shook her head. "I'm not convinced. I want

this creep caught more than anyone. But I just don't think this is him."

Finally Tomlinson spoke. "I trust your gut, Simmons. If you've got doubts, it's probably for good reason.

She glanced over at Greg and almost felt sorry for him. Being one of two detectives to put away a serial killer would be a nice feather in the cap for a new detective. She hated to take it away from him.

Greg stood and walked from the room, and Tomlinson again addressed her.

"Keep working on it. I'm leaving you in charge of the Moorehead case. But remember, the murder investigation is Kaminski's."

"Yes, sir." As she said the words, a pang of guilt passed through her, the sense that she wasn't being totally honest. At the time Tomlinson had reassigned the case, she had already begun the work of locating and contacting Lysandra's sorority sisters. With messages left and searches half completed, it didn't make sense to stop midstream. Kaminski knew, but Tomlinson didn't.

"Sir, when you pulled me from the case, I was in the process of locating Lysandra's sorority sisters. I had already made some contacts and left messages. I'd like permission to continue."

"We've been over this, Simmons." That now-familiar stern tone was back. "I don't want you involved."

"Sir, you're trying to keep me out of harm's way because of my resemblance to Lysandra and my relationship with Kayla. I appreciate that. But all I'm doing is searching databases and making and receiving a few phone calls."

"I know you. You're not going to stop there."

"But I've already proved to you that I will. All those nights I was at Jen's, I never stepped outside, even the night the killer showed up."

Tomlinson leaned back in his chair and crossed his arms, his expression unreadable. But he didn't shut her down. Maybe he was reconsidering.

"I've gotten two return phone calls, and I'm waiting for some others. If it comes down to paying any of them a visit, someone else can do that. But with all the work I've put into this thing in the past six months, please at least let me finish what I've started."

For several moments, Tomlinson didn't speak. Finally he uncrossed his arms and rested them against his desk, shifting his weight forward. "Simmons, you're like a dog with a bone. Once you sink your teeth into something, you won't let it go." Some of the sternness left his gaze, and the hint of a smile touched his mouth. "That's what makes you such a good detective."

Warmth spread through her at his compliment. "So can I finish making these contacts?"

"Finish what you started. Make your phone calls. Talk to your ladies. Then give the information to Kaminski. That had better be the extent of your involvement. Do you understand?"

She couldn't stop the smile that spread across her face. "Yes, sir."

With the leads Lysandra had given them, they were close to solving this thing. She had nine names. Nine women who had had contact with the killer.

One of them was bound to have something that would seal the case up tight.

FOURTEEN

Davis Aluminum wasn't any rinky-dink operation, if the elaborateness of its showroom was any indication. A mini screen enclosure stretched along half of one wall, with a glass room completing the span. The opposite wall held samples of awnings, roofing panels and handrails. Several framed photos filled the space behind the counter, showing off completed pool cages, carports and other product offerings.

Alan stood leaning against the end of one of the shelf units holding bins of screws, washers and other parts and pieces. Lexi roamed the room while a difficult customer harassed the harried clerk behind the counter.

The young woman heaved a sigh. "Sir, the warranties on our carports are for one year. Yours was built over five years ago."

"But it's got dings in the roof."

"That's normal wear and tear. You probably had some hail." She cast a glance at Lexi before returning her gaze to the old man. "How about if I have Mr. Davis call you?"

"You do that."

Alan watched him write down his phone number and make his way to the door with indignant steps. The old guy would be able to plead his case with the boss. Not that it would do him any good. Mr. Davis likely didn't build a successful business by giving away carports.

Lexi approached the counter and Alan stepped up beside her. Technically, she was working the Moorehead stalking case. But there was still that possible link to the murders, something that she would no doubt be pursuing, so he was tagging along.

The young lady flashed them a pleasant smile.

"Sorry about that. That's how it goes. They all run off to lunch and leave me here by myself, and that's when the difficult ones show up. What can I do for you?"

Lexi pulled a notepad and pen from her pocket. "We need to ask you some questions about Wendell Moorehead. He works here, right?"

"Yeah, he's our shop guy. He keeps the floor swept, organizes the materials, helps stage jobs and do inventory, stuff like that. He didn't show up for work yesterday. I heard he's in jail. What did he do?"

"He violated a restraining order, for starters. What can you tell me about him?"

"Well, he's worked for us for four years. He's single. Pretty much keeps to himself."

"Have you ever known him to have a girlfriend?"

"No. It's hard to picture him with a girl."

"Why?"

She shrugged. "I don't know, he just seems socially inept in the picking-up-girls department. He doesn't act very comfortable around women, at least younger, attractive ones."

Alan leaned against the counter. "Has he ever bothered you in any way?"

"No, not at all."

He nodded. She was cute, with a small, upturned nose and faint freckles spattered across her cheeks. But based on what Lexi had told him, "cute" didn't cut it. The girls he stalked were drop-dead gorgeous.

Lexi picked up the line of questioning. "Has he ever asked you out?"

"No."

"Ever done anything that made you feel uncomfortable?"

"Like what?"

"I don't know. Anything. Any inappropriate comments? The way he looks at you?"

"No, not at all. He's more shy than anything."

Lexi tapped her pen on the counter for a moment before continuing, "Davis Aluminum throws a party every October, right?"

"Yeah, a costume party."

"Does Wendell go to these parties?"

"Always. He comes as a cop, even brings a toy pistol and handcuffs. He seems to really get into the part, especially after he's had a couple of drinks. It's as though the costume makes him feel like a ladies' man."

"How so?"

"Not in an obnoxious or creepy way. It's more like it gives him confidence."

"Anything else you can tell us about him?"

"Not that I can think of."

After thanking the clerk, Alan pushed open the glass door and let Lexi walk out ahead of him. Gray clouds were beginning to gather on the western horizon, but it would be some time before Lakeland would benefit from the cooling effect. The sun was high in the sky, reflecting off the black asphalt parking lot and making it feel more like summer than midspring. Of course, between the heat and humidity, Florida felt like summer most of the year.

He let the door swing shut and walked with Lexi to her car. "So what do you think?"

"The same as I did before. He's not our guy."

"I agree." The killer was methodical, organized and highly intelligent. Whatever job he had, it probably wasn't sweeping floors. "So where are you headed off to now?"

"I think I'm going to pay a visit to Jeff Underwood, Moorehead's roommate. You want to come along? I want to see what kind of light he can shed on Moorehead's activities. I also want to know what the two of them were doing with a bottle of chloroform."

"That's a good question."

She unlocked her cruiser and he slid into the passenger seat. "So where do we find this Jeff Underwood?"

"Probably at work. Phil's Tire and Automotive."

When they pulled into the parking lot, the four bay doors were open, with vehicles occupying three of the four slots. Lexi pointed at the end bay.

"That's him there, mounting a tire."

She stepped from the car and headed straight through the bay door, not bothering to use the customer entrance. Two of the mechanics stopped their work to watch them enter. Lexi ignored them and approached Jeff.

"Do you have a few minutes?" She had to shout over the hiss and bang of the tire-changing machine and the high-pitched drone of impact wrenches.

Jeff laid down the crow bar and pulled two foam plugs from his ears, leaving them dangling on the nylon string that circled the back of his neck. "Let's go outside."

He led them around the side of the building to a wooden picnic table that sat on a concrete slab. A light breeze rustled the trees. The storm clouds were gaining mass. If he and Lexi didn't hurry and finish their business, they would probably get wet before the afternoon was over.

Jeff sat on the bench that ran along the back side of the table, and Lexi took a seat opposite him. Alan settled next to her. This was probably where employees sometimes ate their lunches. Or where customers who preferred nature escaped the noise of the television that usually ran from opening to closing in most of these places.

Lexi laid her folded hands on the table. "How long have you and Wendell been roommates?"

"About six months. He's quiet, minds his own business. And he's always on time with the rent."

"I guess you know he's a pretty avid photographer."

"Yeah, he's always heading off somewhere with his camera."

"Has he ever showed you any of his photos?"

"Some."

Lexi nodded. "Lots of women, right?"

"What he's showed me, yeah."

"They look like candid shots, right? Maybe even shots taken without the women being aware."

Jeff shrugged. "I guess so. I didn't pay that much attention."

"Didn't you ever find that odd?"

"What?"

"That he takes pictures of all these women without them knowing anything about it."

"Look, man, I don't get in his business. He can take pictures of whatever he wants."

"The chloroform, is that yours or his?" She shifted gears without a hitch.

Jeff's eyebrows shot up. "Chloroform? Isn't that the stuff they put people out with?"

"Yeah."

"You found chloroform in our place?" He was genuinely surprised, or else he was a good actor.

"Yeah. Is it yours?"

"No way, man. I don't even know where you can buy the stuff."

"You can't. At least not legally." Lexi pushed herself to her feet. "I think that's it for now."

Jeff stood and rounded the table to head back into the garage. "So when can I go home?"

"This evening. They're finishing up this afternoon."

"Good. My buddy's couch doesn't sleep that great."

Lexi flashed him a sympathetic smile. "Thanks for being understanding about the process."

As they walked back toward the car, a gust blew through, carrying the musty scent of rain. It captured some strands of hair that had escaped her braid and laid them across her face. He was tempted to reach up and smooth them back. Instead he stuffed both hands into his pockets.

"Do you think he's lying about the chloroform?"

Lexi shook her head. "I don't think so. The problem is, Wendell doesn't seem to be lying, either. But obviously one of them has to be."

She settled into the driver's seat and he slid in beside her. The murder case was far from wrapped up. The stalking case... Well, it looked like Moorehead was guilty of just that—stalking. And violating a restraining order. If it was anything more, he had covered his tracks well.

Lexi cranked the car and began to back out from the parking space. "Yesterday afternoon I made some progress in the case, but I'm not sure it was in the right direction."

"Oh?"

"I talked to two more of Lysandra's sorority sisters. So that makes a total of four I've located. One was killed in a car accident a couple of years ago. The other three weren't much help. They remember playing tricks on guys, but they don't remember names or descriptions. And they didn't keep photographs."

She braked to a stop at a red light and let her head fall back against the seat. "Now that I'm almost halfway through the list, I'm scared to death that I won't get any more from the last five than I did the first four. Then we'll be back to square one."

She let her head roll to the side, and her gaze slid over to meet his, filled with silent entreaty. A weight had settled over her, its heaviness reflected in her features. His heart clenched.

He lifted a hand to cup her jaw, then caressed her lips with his thumb. "We're going to catch this guy. Someone's going to remember something. Something's going to happen to give us the edge we need. And then we'll nail him."

"I hope you're right. But I just feel like we're missing something."

"Yeah, me, too." He let his fingers linger on her cheek before he lowered his hand.

He had the same gut feeling. They were missing something.

Something important.

Lexi approached the door leading into the station. She had a little paperwork to do and wanted to touch base with Tomlinson. Then her shift would be over.

She released a sigh. It had been a long day and an even longer week. But Friday had finally arrived and the afternoon was drawing to a close. Tonight was her date with Alan. And she was looking forward to it more than she wanted to admit.

He had given her an out by making it nothing more than a meeting to talk shop. Maybe she should have left it at that. That would have been the safer route. Something told her Alan would be ready to jump back into a relationship. So it was up to her to put the brakes on things.

If that was even what she wanted to do. She wasn't so sure anymore.

She enjoyed her independence—no one making demands on her time or trying to control her actions. If she felt like having nachos and dip for dinner instead of cooking, that was what she did. She watched what she wanted to watch on TV without having to discuss her choices with anyone else. She read to relax and played the piano because she wanted to, not because she was pushed to try to fulfill someone else's dream. Independence was great.

It was also lonely.

She swung open the door and navigated her way toward Tomlinson's office. He was there. So was Greg. She hesitated in the open doorway, but her sergeant motioned her inside.

"Come on in. This involves you, too. At least part of it does."

She stepped into the room and nodded a greeting at Greg. He wasn't involved in the murder case. But he was involved in the stalking investigation. And the two cases had become intertwined. At least temporarily.

"Greg was just asking how everything came back on Moorehead."

She sank into the chair. "We've got all kinds of evidence to convict him of stalking."

"What about murder?" The question came from Greg.

"Zilch. Not a shred of evidence in the house and no prints on the chloroform bottle. The biggest find in the Camry was dried-up food. French fries, to be exact."

"So that's it? You're just letting it go?"

She shrugged. "Besides the fact that I don't think he did it, there's nothing linking him to any of the murders."

"What about the chloroform? That's not a common household product, you know."

"No, it's not. But that alone isn't enough to convict him. We've got a Camry that doesn't belong to the suspect and a uniform that's not even the right color. And not a shred of evidence anywhere."

Greg frowned. He obviously didn't agree with her assessment. With his tenacity and determination, he would make a good detective someday. He just needed to learn to look past the obvious and not settle for the easy answers.

Tomlinson leaned back in his chair. "So where are you on everything? Anything new to report?"

"I'm working my way through the list of names Lysandra gave me. One is no longer with us, and three don't remember any details. I think some of these girls did more partying than studying."

Lexi propped her elbows on the arm of the chair and intertwined her fingers over her stomach. "Anyway, I've got five more to talk to. I feel we're right in our assumption that the killer is one of the guys they played tricks on. And Lysandra's Gary is my top pick." Of course, that might not be his name. Lysandra wasn't sure.

"Well, keep me posted."

"I will. I'm hoping that one of these last five women will come up with some good pictures. Lysandra has a great one of this Gary, pink tutu and all. Unfortunately, it's from the back."

She rose from the chair and when she started to follow Greg out the door, Tomlinson's voice stopped her.

"Simmons, I hope you're planning to take the night off."

She stopped and smiled back at him. Over the years, he had accused her more than once of being like a bloodhound on a scent, driving herself relentlessly, refusing to let up.

"I am. Alan and I are going to dinner."

He nodded, his widening smile confirming his approval. "Glad to hear that. I'd love to see you two work through whatever's come between you."

Heat crept up her neck and into her cheeks. Had Alan discussed his personal life with Tomlinson? Or theirs?

"No one told me anything," he said, as if he had read her thoughts. "No one needed to. I can see it in your eyes every time you mention him. And I hear it in his voice every time he talks about you. Let it go, Lexi. Life's too short to not embrace a chance at love when it comes our way."

She nodded, then escaped down the hall. That was easy for him to say. He had been happily married for thirty years. Most of the people she knew weren't that lucky.

Like her parents. They must have been wildly in love at some point. But whatever zeal they had experienced in their early years had cooled to mere tolerance.

If that was the kind of life she had to look forward to, she would just stay single.

* * *

Lexi stepped out of the door of Louie Mack's Steakhouse, her fingers entwined with Alan's. A live band serenaded the diners seated on the patio, and a barely-there breeze whispered through the trees, bringing cooling relief to what would otherwise be a stuffy evening.

She would have been content with Pappy's, but Alan had insisted on taking her somewhere special. If he was striving for the ultimate romantic evening, he had succeeded. Everything was perfect. They had eaten inside, served by a tuxedoed waiter and bathed in the soft glow of dimmed wall sconces. A single votive candle burned in the center of each of the linen-draped tables, and orchestral music formed a soothing backdrop to their dinner conversation.

She stopped at the passenger side of Alan's Mustang and waited for him to open the door. "Thank you for a perfect evening. I'm glad we made it a date instead of a business meeting."

He smiled down at her. "Me, too."

All evening long, their conversation had consisted of lighthearted banter and lots of reminiscing, but not one word about the case. It had been a nice reprieve.

"So who are the bad boys of Harmony Grove now?" According to Alan, the troublemakers they had grown up with had finally straightened out. Or were in prison.

Alan slid into the driver's seat and started the car.

"When mischief happens now, Duncan Alcott is usually at the center of it."

"He's got it pretty rough at home."

"I know. So far it's been minor stuff. You know, skipping school, vandalism, getting into his dad's liquor stash. The problem is, he's a leader and an instigator."

"And you're trying to keep him from corrupting the other kids." She smiled over at him. The epitome of the humble public servant, he took a personal interest in all of Harmony Grove's citizens, especially its troubled youth.

Alan nodded. "I'm holding out hope for him, though. A month or so ago, a new family moved to Harmony Grove. Their sixteen-year-old daughter has caught his eye. She's a good girl, and I think she's made him her project. Nothing like a pretty girl to turn a guy's world upside down."

He glanced over at her, his gaze filled with meaning. He was no longer thinking about the newcomer. He was thinking about her. Her stomach made a funny little flip before settling into a pool of warmth.

He had certainly turned her world upside down. Several times. Way back when she'd first fallen for him, head over heels, and now, all these years later, every time he looked at her a certain way. In the wake of hours spent working side by side, culminating in a romantic dinner out, all her reasons for maintaining her independence suddenly seemed lame.

When Alan braked to a stop next to her Mazda, she wasn't ready for the evening to be over.

"It's probably too late for a movie. And we already had dessert at Louie Mack's. So I don't have an excuse to invite you in."

He grinned over at her. "I think I need to say hi to the cats. I mean, they haven't seen me in what, four days?"

She returned his smile. "Then you're definitely overdue."

Evidently Suki thought so, too. As soon as they stepped inside, she was in the entry, weaving between their legs and hollering up at them. Alan bent to pick her up and the meows instantly turned to purrs.

"Didn't you feed them before we left?"

"Of course I did. Those weren't hunger cries. She was letting us know she didn't appreciate being neglected for almost three hours."

"A little demanding, isn't she?" He bent to put her back on the floor. "So when can we do this again?"

"What? Louie Mack's?" She grinned up at him.

"Louie Mack's two or three times a week might be a little pricey. I was thinking more along the lines of a movie. Tomorrow night, maybe?"

"Two dates in one weekend?"

"I'll make it three if you'll agree to Sunday, too."

She shook her head, still grinning. "What's that going to do to your playboy reputation? All your other lady friends are going to feel neglected."

He stepped toward her and rested both hands on

her shoulders. "There's only one lady I care about. And she's standing right in front of me."

His eyes held an earnestness that caught her off guard, and her own teasing smile slid away. She had wanted to take things slow. But with him looking at her that way, she was ready to throw away all her resolutions and fall head over heels in love.

She moistened her lips. A kiss would be the perfect end to a perfect evening. Alan was thinking the same thing. She could see it in his eyes.

He leaned closer, slowly enough to give her ample opportunity to avoid his kiss. But she didn't turn away. Instead she slid her arms around his neck and tilted her face upward, welcoming his advance. A moment later his lips met hers, gently at first, then with more pressure. She had wondered if the spark would still be there. She needn't have worried. It was there and then some, as if it had been held on a slow simmer for all those years, ready to ignite when the conditions were right.

And tonight they were right.

Love surged up from within, so powerful it almost made her dizzy. Maybe it had been there all along, buried in some remote corner of her heart, kept under lock and key. Whatever its source, she could no longer deny it. She loved Alan, and regardless of what she might have to give up, she no longer wanted to live her life without him.

All too soon, he ended the kiss and stepped back

to put some distance between them. "Tomorrow night, then?"

She forced a casual smile. He didn't seem nearly as affected as she was. "Tomorrow night."

"And Sunday?"

"We'll see. You might be tired of me by then."

"Never."

She followed him to the door and watched him walk to his car. Minutes later her cell phone rang. *Unavailable* stretched across the screen and a seed of uneasiness sprouted inside her. She pressed the phone to her ear and breathed a tentative, "Hello?"

"Alexis." The hoarse whisper raised the hair on the back of her neck and sent goose bumps cascading over her skin.

"Who is this?"

The caller continued in the same hoarse tone, making the voice impossible to identify. "I've warned you before, and I'm warning you one last time. Back off, or you're next. And don't think you can evade me. I know where you live."

The phone clicked dead. A chill swept over her and a knot of fear settled in her gut. How had he found her, and where did he get her phone number?

She marched to the end table and dropped her phone back into her purse. He hadn't found her. He was bluffing. He'd gotten her name and number from one of the flyers that she and Alan had passed out. As far as he was concerned, she was nothing but a name on a piece of paper. He didn't know where she lived.

Determination coursed through her. Five women had been murdered, with another living in fear. All six deserved justice. And she wasn't going to let some idle threats keep her from doing her part to give it to them, as small as that part might be.

At least Alan hadn't been there to witness the call. And she wouldn't tell him about it. If she did, it would only end badly.

But maybe she needed to tell him. This wasn't the first risk she had taken, and it wouldn't be the last. If they hoped to have any kind of relationship, he was going to have to accept what she did and the danger that went with it.

If he couldn't, they would have to part ways.

And she would rather it be sooner than later.

FIFTEEN

Alan eased to a stop in the Cornerstone Community Church parking lot, two spaces over from an ancient, faded blue Impala.

Duncan Alcott at church? *No way.*

But in Harmony Grove, the blue bomb was one of a kind. Maybe even in all of Polk County.

He turned off the car and opened his door to the gong of the church bell. The sky was cloudless, the sun midway to its peak, promising another warm spring day. Parishioners filed into the small brick building topped by a white steeple.

Halfway to the covered porch, he glanced back at the Impala. The driver still sat inside, slouched down as if he didn't want to be seen.

Alan turned around and headed back in the direction from which he had come. With an SUV parked between them, he hadn't noticed Duncan before. Now that he had, he couldn't in all good conscience go in and enjoy the service knowing Duncan would be outside, probably breaking into cars.

Duncan watched him approach but didn't roll down the window until Alan tapped on it.

"Morning, Duncan. What are you doing?"

"I'm waiting for someone."

"You're waiting in the church parking lot." He didn't try to keep the skepticism out of his voice.

"No way am I going in there by myself."

Alan lifted his brows. "You're here to attend services?"

"What else would I be here for?"

No, he wasn't going to answer that. At least not out loud. "All right, then. I'll see you inside."

He turned to head back toward the front of the church and had to wait for a gold Lexus to pass. A familiar figure sat in the backseat, face framed in the window, waving enthusiastically. She was the new girl, the same one he had caught in the tree with Duncan. And probably the reason Duncan would be sitting in church on a Sunday morning instead of roaming the streets looking for trouble.

A glance back at the Impala confirmed his suspicions. Duncan was getting out of the car.

When Alan walked into the church, Roger Tandy met him at the door. At somewhere just shy of sixty, he was a fixture there, had taught every Sunday school class at one point or another and had held several positions on the board. Now he was an usher and made sure that no one got into Cornerstone Community Church without a firm handshake and a welcoming smile.

Alan moved up the aisle and scanned those seated until he found Chief Dalton and his wife, Jess. He slid into the pew and took a seat on the end. For the past month he had avoided sitting with any of the hopeful single ladies. He had also pretty well given up his social life, except for what involved Lexi. But that was all right. Since she'd come back into his life, he hadn't wanted to see anyone else.

He had just gotten comfortable and was enjoying the band's warm-up to worship when a tentative tap on the shoulder called for his attention.

"May I join you?"

When he looked up into Lexi's face, his heart made a little stutter. She was beautiful. Her hair was down, flowing over her shoulders like golden silk, and her lips, touched with pink gloss, were turned upward in a shy smile.

"Of course." He stood and guided her into the space between him and Shane.

It was obviously the day for unexpected guests. In the row opposite theirs, Duncan Alcott sat nestled between the new girl and her father, looking as if breathing might somehow bring down the wrath of God. Hopefully, Lexi would be a little more comfortable.

She settled in next to him. "Yeah, I'm here. I can tell that all this is important to you. I figure if there's going to be anything between us, I'd better check it out."

"I'm glad you did." He had invited her last night, after a movie and a walk in the park. But she hadn't given him much hope that she would come. But here she was, an answer to his prayers. Actually, he'd had a lot of those lately.

The worship band segued into a familiar chorus, the change in volume signaling the start of the service, and the people rose to their feet. As the songs progressed from one to the next, Lexi's eyes never left the lyrics displayed on the screen at the front. Her lips moved, but whatever came out was too soft for him to hear.

Even Duncan attempted to sing along. Alan had cast some quick glances that direction and found him much like Lexi, eyes glued to the screen. More than likely, his participation was for the sole purpose of trying to impress his new girlfriend. But it was a start.

When the service was over, Alan led Lexi toward the door. Twenty minutes later they emerged into the sunshine after being greeted by two-thirds of the membership of Cornerstone. One thing was certain: they were a friendly bunch.

"So what did you think?"

She nodded. "I liked it. I think I'll be back."

"Good." He scanned the parking lot for the blue Mazda and found it near the back. "How about lunch?"

"Okay, but this time it's my treat. I've got a bunch of homemade chili simmering in the Crock-Pot."

"Mmm, sounds yummy." He remembered her chili. She was a good cook even back then.

She pressed the key fob and the locks clicked open. "So I'll see you at my place in about twenty minutes."

Before she could get into the car, a sound stopped her, the buzz of a phone set on vibrate. She stiffened, and concern flashed across her features. But the moment she looked at the screen, the tension fled her body. She released a pent-up breath. "Oh, it's Mom."

He watched her while she explained that no, she wouldn't be there today, that she had already made plans, but she would stop by tomorrow evening after work. She ended the call and he eyed her with suspicion.

"Since when are you relieved to see that it's your mom calling?"

She shrugged and slid into the seat. "You just never know."

"What are you not telling me?"

She hesitated, as if trying to decide how, or whether, to answer him. Finally she sighed. "I got a call from the killer. Or at least someone posing as the killer."

Fire shot through his veins, spurred by a fierce sense of protectiveness. "Were you going to tell me about this at some point?"

"Yes, I was. I just hadn't gotten around to it yet. It only happened Friday night."

Friday night. They were together all evening Saturday and she'd failed to mention it. But chastising her would only make her clam up.

"So what did he say?"

"He said he warned me before, and that if I don't back off, I'm next."

The fire turned to cold fury, lacing his words with flint. "Anything else?"

"He said he knows where I live."

He clenched his fists, fighting for control. When he finally allowed himself to speak, the words came out sharper than he intended. "Are you ready now to go stay with your mom?"

She crossed her arms in a gesture of stubbornness. "I'd rather fight fire-breathing dragons."

"Then stay with me. I have a guest room."

"Look, he doesn't know where I live. He's bluffing."

"Then how did he get your phone number?"

"The flyers we passed out. They've got my name and cell number at the bottom."

He sucked in a stabilizing breath. What she said made sense. But still…

"Please go stay with someone." He reached out to squeeze her shoulder. "Don't take unnecessary chances. You don't have anything to prove."

She jerked away from him. "Is that what you think, that I'm trying to prove something? Look, Alan, this is my job. There's risk. As a police officer yourself, you should understand it better than anyone."

He did understand. He took those risks, too. But watching the woman he loved put herself in danger was a different story. "I'm just worried about you."

"I appreciate that. But I'm well trained and I'm

careful. You're going to have to trust me." She uncrossed her arms and let her hands lie in her lap. When she looked back up at him, her eyes were filled with sadness. "If you can't cope with what I do, then maybe we need to end this right here."

Pain stabbed through him at her words. No, he couldn't lose her again. He would do whatever it took to make it work.

He reached out to cup her cheek. "I walked away once. I'm not making that mistake again."

She put her hand over his and closed her eyes. "You're not the only one who walked away."

No, they had both made mistakes. But now they were being given a second chance. He just had to come to grips with the dangers she faced every day and the fact that he wouldn't always be there to protect her.

He heaved a sigh of resignation.

Things were much simpler when she was just a business major.

Lexi walked toward the briefing room feeling almost weightless. Life was good. She had spent most of her weekend with Alan, each hour reminding her of all the reasons she had fallen in love with him to begin with. He even seemed to be coming to terms with the danger inherent in her job.

If all that wasn't reason enough to celebrate, yesterday evening after Alan left, she had made some more phone calls and hit the jackpot. One of Lysandra's sorority sisters had photos. Lots of them. Tonight she was tied up, but promised that tomorrow night she would be happy to pull out every album she possessed.

Lexi released a contented sigh. With actual photos to circulate, it would only be a matter of time until someone recognized the killer and called in a tip. They were so close.

Yes, life was good. Gratitude swelled inside and she sent a silent thank-you heavenward. Alan was rubbing off on her. And that wasn't a bad thing. After all, she had spent so many years blaming God for the bad things in her life that it was only fair to credit Him with the good. That didn't mean she was ready to go all religious. She knew the way. She had attended church enough times as a child. But she didn't commit to something until she was ready.

She headed down the hall and several detectives filed into the briefing room ahead of her, Greg among them. Maybe she would suggest that Tomlinson let him accompany whoever Kaminski sent on the visit tomorrow night. She remembered what it was like being brand-new, longing to prove herself. Greg so wanted to catch this guy. Being part of the final interview that would bring him down would mean a lot.

She walked into the room and took a seat next to Kaminski. She hadn't had a chance yet to bring him up to speed on what she had learned last night. Other than a brief, excited call to Alan, she hadn't told anyone, even Tomlinson.

The sergeant took his place at the front of the room and delivered a quick rundown of the events of the past few days. Finally he stepped out from behind the podium and addressed Kaminski. "Anything new to report on your end?"

Kaminski shifted in the chair next to her. "Nothing new since last week. We pursued a couple of leads that turned out to be dead ends."

"Simmons, what about you? Any luck locating those roommates?"

"Actually, yes, last night. I haven't even had a chance to fill Kaminski in on it yet." She flashed the detective next to her an apologetic smile. It wasn't necessary. Secure in his years of service to the department, he didn't view her as competition. They were working toward the same end.

"I made contact with Ashley Rittman. Talked to her for quite a while. She had some pretty interesting stories. She and her sisters always looked for some incoming freshman who had *gullible* written all over him, and then they went to work scheming. She remembers all these guys."

Lexi leaned forward and continued, excitement in her tone. "She's got photos, lots of them. All the guys they played tricks on. She doesn't specifically remember the name Gary. She says she's terrible with names. But the pink tutu was unforgettable."

Some snickers rippled through the room and one of the detectives gave a grunt of protest. "We're hunting for guys in ski masks and hoodies while you're chasing nut jobs in tutus. You Homicide people get to have all the fun."

She ignored the ribbing and continued, "She's got great shots of all these guys. As far as I'm concerned, every one of them is a suspect. But based on what Lysandra said, I'm putting this Gary character at the top of my list. I'm meeting with Ashley tomorrow night. She lives way down in Bonita Springs, but something tells me it's going to be worth the drive."

Tomlinson nodded. "Good job, Simmons."

When he dismissed everyone, Greg held back. After everyone except Tomlinson had filed out, Greg approached her.

"Congratulations. It sounds like you've made a breakthrough."

"That's what I'm hoping. I guess we'll find out tomorrow night."

"Would you like company?"

"Actually, I won't be going." She glanced at Tomlinson but knew better than to even ask. "You still might be able to tag along with whoever does, though. What do you think, Sarge?"

"I'll talk to Kaminski, since he's in charge. But I don't see a problem with it."

Greg crossed his arms, taking a firm stance. "I think you should do this last interview." He shifted his gaze to Tomlinson. "This is our big break, and Lexi's been with this thing from the beginning. It seems only fair."

Tomlinson fixed narrowed eyes on her. "Did you put him up to this?"

Greg spoke before she had a chance to respond. "No, she didn't. I'm sticking up for her on my own. She's been awesome to work with. She's a good detective and a great mentor."

She offered him an appreciative smile, tamping down a twinge of guilt over the mental grumbling she had done when Tomlinson had first paired her with him. Not that she expected it to do any good, but it was nice of him to go to bat for her.

Tomlinson shook his head. "Greg, you can go, but Lexi stays. Until this guy is locked away, she remains behind the scenes."

Greg nodded. "All right. But if you'll consider changing your mind, I promise I won't let anything happen to her."

When she walked from the room, Greg followed. Within moments, he was next to her.

"Thanks for suggesting that I go along."

She dipped her head. "And thanks for sticking up for me."

"I hope Tomlinson reconsiders. But whoever talks to the girl, I'll be happy to chauffeur. In fact, give me the address, and I'll have it all programmed into my GPS."

She made her way down the hall with a spring in her step. She couldn't help but feel the same excitement, regardless of who got to do the final interviews and eventually bring in the killer. After six long months, it was almost over.

"Follow me to my desk and I'll copy it down for you."

He walked through her cubicle opening and waited while she retrieved a pen and paper. "I'm as anxious to see those pictures as you are. We're finally ready to bring this guy to justice." He flashed her an easy smile. "After all, that's what this job is all about, isn't it? Justice."

Lexi slouched against the back of the couch, feet propped on the coffee table and a distorted image frozen on the television screen. She had been half through her movie when Alan phoned. If he had a reason for calling, he hadn't told her yet what it was. So far, it had all been small talk.

"I miss you."

The lost-puppy-dog tone made her smile. "We were just together yesterday."

"That was yesterday. This is today. After three straight days of seeing you, I think I'm going through withdrawal."

"You know, you're getting dangerously close to pathetic territory."

"Hey, I can't help it if I'm crazy about you."

"You know what? I'm glad…even if you are pathetic." As much as she teased him, she had been pretty pathetic all day herself.

"So what are you up to other than watching a movie, which I so rudely interrupted?"

"Tonight, that's it. Then tomorrow night, there's a slim chance that I'll be going to see Ashley Rittman."

"A slim chance?"

"More like microscopic. Greg is trying to talk Tomlinson into letting me go talk to her. I suggested that, whoever does it, Tomlinson let Greg go along. He seems like he wants to solve this thing as badly as I do." She sighed and switched the phone to her other ear. "He was so convinced the killer was Wendell Moorehead that he was ready to go after him full-bore. His enthusiasm and determination are definitely there. He just needs a little direction."

"Well, if anyone can give it to him, you can."

The doorbell rang, cutting off her response. A hollow coldness spread throughout her body, holding her frozen in the chair as surely as if she had been bound. Despite the presence of all three of her cats, her solitude was more pronounced than ever.

"Was that the doorbell I just heard?" The fear in Alan's voice reflected her own.

"Yeah."

"Don't open the door. Call 9-1-1. I'll be there as fast as I can. Whatever you do, don't open the door."

She swallowed hard and pushed her body into gear. It could be a neighbor needing to borrow something. She glanced at her watch. At ten o'clock at night? Not likely.

"I need to at least look through the peephole before I get the police out here."

"Just call 9-1-1." His tone was filled with urgency. "In view of the threats you've gotten, you shouldn't go anywhere near that door."

"If it's the killer, he's not going to shoot me through the door. That's not his M.O." She stepped into the entry and moved slowly toward the door, then dropped her voice to a whisper. "Stay on the phone with me."

She moved closer. Six feet to go. He was just on the other side of the door. But he wouldn't know she was there. The porch light was on and the entry light was off.

Four feet. Shooting through the door wasn't his M.O. But she wasn't just another potential victim. She had been warned. Would he shoot her just to get her out of the way?

Two feet. The bell rang again and she stifled a startled shriek. Her hand went to her chest and she willed her heart rate to slow.

She took another step and leaned in toward the door. Peepholes were one way. And with the light off inside, there wouldn't even be a shadow. She pressed her face to the door.

No police uniform.

Relief washed over her and her gaze swept upward to his face.

"Oh, it's just Greg." The last of the tension fled her body.

"Why would Greg show up on your doorstep at ten

o'clock at night?" Her relief obviously didn't transfer to Alan. Suspicion was heavy in his tone.

"Maybe Tomlinson gave in."

"He could call to tell you that."

"Maybe he wanted to tell me in person. I mean, I wouldn't think anything of *you* showing up at ten at night."

"That's different."

"Trust me. If he has anything in mind other than the case, he'll find out really fast that I'm taken." The possibility that he was there for any kind of romantic purpose was highly unlikely. He had made it clear that he was quite happy just him and his dog. Alan had nothing to worry about.

"I'll call you back." She disconnected the call before he could protest further and slid the phone into her back pocket. Alan would just have to stew for a few minutes. Whatever Greg's reason for coming, he wouldn't be there long.

She opened the door about twelve inches. Greg stood on her porch, a Jeep in the driveway behind him.

"You *are* here." The smile he gave her didn't quite reach his eyes. "I was beginning to wonder if you were home. Can I come in?"

A wave of uneasiness swept over her and she wasn't sure why. She should probably have grabbed her weapon. No, that was ridiculous. He was a fellow detective.

"It's pretty late. What did you need?"

"I had some things to talk to you about, things related to the case."

Her gaze swept over him and her uneasiness intensified. He was turned just enough so she couldn't see his right hand.

"How about if we discuss this tomorrow?"

"I was really hoping to talk to you tonight."

He took a step closer and she tried to slam the door. Just shy of closing, it suddenly exploded inward. A scream rose in her throat but never made it to her mouth. With lightning speed, Greg burst through the opening, spun her against him and pressed something over her face.

A sweet-smelling white cloth.

Panic careened through her system and her pulse jumped to double time, pounding out its erratic rhythm.

Greg was the killer.

How could she have missed that?

She clasped her hands and thrust her arms out and up, breaking his hold. In one smooth motion she spun and kneed him in the groin.

She didn't wait to assess the damage. A grunt and a muttered curse followed her as she flew into the living room. He should have known better than to accost a woman trained in self-defense. His other victims would have panicked and pulled on his hands, struggling unsuccessfully to loosen bands of steel. But she knew better. She wouldn't try to use sheer strength against someone eight inches taller and a hundred pounds heavier.

Now if she could just reach the back door.

The vase in the entry crashed to the tile floor and heavy footsteps pounded behind her. The next second, rough hands against her shoulder blades sent her hurtling forward, facedown on the carpet. Before she knew what had happened, he had flipped her onto her back and straddled her, arms pinned beneath his knees. The cloth once again came down across her face, and no matter how she bucked and twisted, she couldn't break free.

She held her breath, still fighting with every ounce of strength she had left. If she could just throw him off her, she would stand a chance. Not a big one, but more than she would pinned to the floor. But he was too strong and too heavy.

Her lungs burned, the urge to inhale overshadowing all else, until she finally gulped in those coveted breaths of air. But they were tainted. Sickeningly sweet. The room seemed to stretch and blur, shifting slowly to one side, then the other, as Greg's face came in and out of focus.

Suki watched from the end of the hall. Lexi couldn't see her, but she could hear her, yowling in the low, plaintive cry of the Siamese. Midnight and Itsy were probably hiding. What would happen to them when she was gone? Her mother was too selfish to care for anyone but herself. Maybe Alan would take them.

She should have listened to him. All the times he'd

pleaded with her to stay somewhere else and she'd stubbornly refused. Now what he feared most was coming to pass. He would be devastated. *I'm sorry, sweetheart. I love you.*

The grogginess intensified and the cat's cries grew farther and farther away. Nausea swept over her, wave after wave, until she would almost welcome the sweet comfort of oblivion.

Her eyes no longer wanted to stay open. The room faded into the distance. And so did Greg. He was wearing a grimace. Or maybe it was a smile. She wasn't sure.

Her eyes drifted shut and refused to open.

SIXTEEN

Alan sat in his recliner clicking through the channels. The thought of Greg being with Lexi shouldn't bother him. But it did. What business did he have showing up at her house at ten o'clock at night? Sure, they worked together. But something about it just didn't sit right with him.

Maybe if he knew the guy, it would be different. But he had never met him. He was just a name, a faceless man in a uniform.

And he was alone with Lexi. At her house. Late at night.

He laid down the remote and picked up his phone. After staring at the screen for several moments, he put it back on the end table.

No, she'd said she would call as soon as Greg left. It had only been ten minutes. If he called her back now, he would come across as a jealous boyfriend.

But he couldn't shake the dread that had blanketed him the moment he'd heard the ring of her doorbell through the phone. *Lord, please protect her. Help me to put her in Your hands and leave her there.*

He tipped back his head and closed his eyes, willing himself to relax. When that didn't work, he once again picked up the remote. If nothing sparked his interest during ten minutes of channel surfing, it probably wouldn't now, either. But at least it gave him something to do.

But it wasn't enough. He pushed himself up from the chair and started to pace. She should have called by now, if to say nothing more than that everything was fine and she and Greg were having a powwow. She knew how concerned he was. The least she could do was call.

He looked at his watch for the hundredth time. Twenty minutes. Plenty of time for Greg to say whatever he'd needed to say.

Unless he was hitting on her. Refusing to take no for an answer.

He snatched up the phone and redialed her number. So she would think he was acting like a jealous boyfriend. And Greg would, too. So be it. He had to make sure she wasn't in some kind of trouble.

The phone rang once, twice. "Come on, Lexi, pick up." A third ring. He clutched the phone more tightly. She often left it on vibrate, forgetting to turn the ring volume back up after a meeting. If she'd laid it down somewhere and it was still on vibrate, she might not hear it.

After the fourth ring her message came on and he disconnected the call.

He laid down the phone and resumed his pacing. Greg was a cop. As much as he didn't like the idea of her alone with him late at night, she was as safe with him as she would be with anybody.

So why the sense of dread? Why the persistent feeling that something was horribly wrong?

He froze midstep, his blood turning to ice in his veins.

What if the killer isn't someone impersonating a cop? What if he is a cop?

What if the killer was Greg?

He grabbed his keys, pistol and Bluetooth and ran for the door, dialing Tomlinson as he went. Judging from the slurred "Hello?" the sergeant had been sleeping. Hopefully the man would wake up fast, because Alan didn't have the time or patience to ease into the conversation. He backed from the driveway and sped away, leaving a long path of rubber and probably several annoyed neighbors.

"What kind of car does Greg drive?"

"Greg who?" Tomlinson's words were still laced with the remnants of sleep.

"The detective who's been working with Lexi. What does he drive?"

"A Jeep."

"Does he have a second vehicle?"

"I don't know. I've only known him to drive the

Jeep. Why? What's going on?" Tomlinson sounded fully awake now.

"I'm on my way to Lexi's. I think the killer might be Greg."

There was a long silence on the other end of the line. Finally Tomlinson spoke. "Are you sure?"

"Not a hundred percent. But I was on the phone with her and Greg showed up at her house. She was going to call me as soon as he left. That was almost a half hour ago."

"Have you tried to call her?"

"She's not answering."

"I'll put out an APB on the Jeep and the white Camry. And I'll send units to Lexi's. I'm also going to see what vehicles are registered to Greg. Call me as soon as you get there."

"I will. And call me as soon as you learn anything."

By the time he pulled onto Lexi's street, sirens sounded in the distance, screaming ever closer. Moments later, two Auburndale P.D. cruisers followed him into her drive, sirens silenced but lights still flashing.

Alan jumped from the car and ran toward the house.

"Freeze!"

The command stopped him in his tracks and he turned slowly, hands raised. Two pistols were trained on him.

"Alan White, Harmony Grove P.D. I initiated the call."

Both guns went back into their holsters and the officers approached.

"We were told you were on the way. We didn't expect you to beat us here."

He pounded hard on the door. He wouldn't touch the bell. Greg knew enough to use a knuckle or a gloved hand, so there probably weren't any prints, but he wasn't taking a chance. His knock went unanswered.

One of the officers walked to his car and returned with a pair of latex gloves. He tried the door then dropped his hand.

"Locked."

Locked up tight and lights off.

Just as with the other victims.

"Do you have a key?"

He shook his head. They hadn't gotten that far yet. In fact, they were just getting started. *Lord, please don't let me lose her already.*

He stood back and thrust outward with one foot. The door exploded inward; the strike-plate side of the jamb splintered. Across the entry, a vase lay shattered on the tiled floor, evidence of a struggle.

The kitchen was untouched. So was the living room. Suki sat in the middle of the floor, mouth open in a mournful cry that shredded his already frayed nerves. Itsy waited in the hall, watching him with wide green eyes. Midnight was probably too freaked out to show himself. If only cats could talk.

His cell phone rang and he took the call, moving down the hall toward the bedrooms.

"Are you at Lexi's?" It was Tomlinson.

"Yeah. I'm inside now. As near as we can tell, she's gone."

A heavy sigh came through the phone. "I guessed as much. I got the info on the vehicles, and it's not good."

Alan closed his eyes and steeled himself for what he knew he was going to hear.

"There are two vehicles registered to Greg. One is a 2005 Jeep. The other is a 2002 Toyota Camry, white."

Alan expelled a breath that he hadn't realized he had been holding. If there had been any doubt, the slightest chance that this was all a misunderstanding, Tomlinson's words shattered that possibility in an instant.

"We'll find her, Alan. We've got law enforcement from all agencies combing the county."

Alan nodded and swallowed the lump in his throat. "Her phone doesn't seem to be here. Which means it might be on her. Alert emergency 9-1-1 in case she gets to use it."

He moved back to the front of the house and stepped out the door. "And check all the wooded areas near Auburndale. If he stays consistent, he'll take her somewhere nearby. I'll have the two officers here question the neighbors, see if they saw anything." Although it wasn't likely. The houses were all dark.

"What are you going to do?"

"I'm going to look for her."

His chances of finding one lone vehicle in the dark, probably hidden in the woods, weren't very good.

But knowing the way this guy worked, he wouldn't kill her right away. He would wait until she revived. Then he would begin his photo shoot, bruising and bloodying her up a little between each shot. The thought drove a red-hot poker through his heart.

But it also lifted a touch of his despair. The killer could take as much time as he wanted.

Because as long as she was alive, there was hope.

Lexi squeezed her eyes shut, trying to block out the pain throbbing through her head. If this was what it felt like to wake up after a night of wild partying, she didn't see the appeal. No amount of fun was worth this.

But she hadn't had any fun. Not that she could remember anyway. So why did she feel so rotten?

Her hip hurt. So did her upper arm. She was lying on something. She tried to shift her position and a moan escaped through her nose.

Sounds nearby filtered into her consciousness— the rustle of clothing and the crack of twigs. Her eyes fluttered open. She wasn't home in bed. In fact, she was outside. Pine needles lay all around, providing little cushion for what she now knew were exposed roots.

"Well, well, well."

The familiar male voice sent awareness crashing

down on her, as violent as a landslide. Panic spiraled through her, constricting her throat and making it hard to breathe. The killer was Greg. Lysandra had said his name was Gary. But she also said she wasn't sure. Gary…Greg. She was close.

"I'm glad you finally decided to come around. It's no fun without you."

She tried to sit up, but couldn't move her arms. Ropes cutting into her wrists told her that her hands were tied behind her back. Her ankles were restrained, too, and something covered her mouth. Duct tape, she guessed.

Greg leaned over her and she shrank away from him. But instead of hitting or kicking her, he pulled her to a seated position. She looked around, trying to determine her location. A three-quarter moon shone bright white in a sparsely clouded sky. Trees stood all around, mostly scrub oaks and pines.

He stepped back and moved slowly around her, like a lion circling its prey. He was dressed in jeans and a red polo shirt, and a camera hung around his neck. The uniform he'd worn with the other victims hadn't been necessary. She'd let him in without it.

How could she have been so gullible? She was trained. She had good instincts. She had interacted with Greg over and over and never once suspected anything. She had been careless, blind and stupid. And it might cost her her life.

Stop it! Berating herself was accomplishing nothing. She needed to focus her efforts on staying alive.

"You just had to keep pushing, didn't you?" He continued to circle her. "You couldn't just let it go. I was ready to call it even. I was only halfway through my list, but after almost getting caught, I decided to consider the price paid. I can do that, you know. I have the authority to mete out the punishment, and I have the authority to offer pardon, to declare the debt paid. That's what the uniform is all about. Justice."

Dread trickled over her at his words, so eerily reminiscent of the ones he had spoken at the station. He stopped pacing to stand over her, blocking the moon from view and intensifying her sense of vulnerability.

"It would have been all over. No one else needed to die. I even gave you the perfect out, someone to pin the crimes on and declare the case solved."

He'd given her the perfect out? What was he talking about? He hadn't had anything to do with Wendell's arrest.

Her eyes widened as realization slammed into her. Greg had nothing to do with the arrest, but he was involved in the investigation, which gave him the opportunity to plant the chloroform. That was why it had taken him so long to get back after picking up lunch and dropping off Jeff —he'd made a trip home first.

And when he got back to Wendell's, he'd gone straight to the bathroom to wash his hands. That was when he'd slipped the bottle under the sink.

Greg began to pace back and forth in front of her. "I gave you every opportunity to back off. I even warned you. Twice. And you ignored me." He looked over at her, shaking his head, his expression scolding. "Not a wise decision. Because look where it got you."

Yeah, bound and gagged. Helpless. A wave of despair threatened to engulf her, and she fought to hold it back, clinging to a sliver of hope. Alan knew she was with Greg. He would have tried to call her. And when she didn't answer, he would have figured out Greg was the killer. By now, he would have alerted all the agencies. There was probably already a massive search under way.

Greg stepped back and lifted the camera to his face. The next moment the flash blinded her and she flinched.

"It's all good, though. I'm getting to kill two birds with one stone." He gave her a devious grin. "Pardon the pun."

He moved to the side of her and she followed him with her gaze.

"Look straight ahead. I'm trying to get a side shot."

Her eyes widened and she continued to stare at him. He was expecting her to pose for his photo shoot? He was nuts. But he snapped the picture anyway and again started to pace.

"Anyway, as I was saying, it's all working out beautifully. Good things come to him who plans." He smiled at his twist of the well-known proverb. "Not only will I get you off my back, but I'll have the satisfaction of once again seeing justice done. Nothing gives me greater joy. It's why I went into law enforcement. To see wrongs atoned for. Tonight you're paying for Lysandra's sins." He tipped his head back and spread his arms. "Justice. Oh, sweet justice."

A chill swept over her, seeping into her bones. He was nuts. His warped sense of right and wrong wasn't justice. He was a vigilante, but worse, because he preyed on the innocent.

When he looked back down at her, his smile faded instantly. He narrowed his gaze and took a threatening step closer. "Don't look at me like I'm crazy. Because I'm not. This has been done all through the ages—the innocent sacrificed so someone else can live. I'm sure you know the stories. The people offering a young virgin to the dragon so the village can have peace and protection. Children being sacrificed to appease the gods. That principle is even at the foundation of Christianity—Jesus Christ dying for the sins of the world."

He snapped a third picture and continued to talk. "What's really nice, though, is that, thanks to your expert sleuthing, all these women are learning that others have died for their actions. They'll carry that knowledge all the way to their graves. That's the sweetest revenge of all."

He leaned over her again, but this time he drew back a fist and slammed it into her left cheek. The blow came so suddenly, she didn't have a chance to prepare. It knocked her to the side and she rolled onto her back, panic pounding up her spine. Pain throbbed through the side of her face and faded spots of light seemed to dance in the sky above her.

It was all starting. The abuse that each of the other victims had experienced. The gruesome photo shoot. Then strangulation. And more photos. But she wouldn't be there to experience them.

God, please help me.

She struggled to quell the rising panic. Alan was looking for her. So were others, people who cared for her and would do everything in their power to find her before it was too late.

But no one knew where to look. She didn't even know where she was. The wall of despair rolled closer.

"Sit up." His tone held an icy edge.

When she didn't respond immediately, she was rewarded with a boot in the ribs. A half moan, half grunt escaped through her nose.

"I said sit up."

She struggled to comply. He circled behind her to put two hands under her arms and drag her backward. Something caught for a second, an object in her back pocket. Once he had propped her against a tree, she slid her bound hands over the curve of her bottom, where they met a hard rectangular object. Hope surged through her and her heart began to pound.

Greg hadn't taken her phone. Since it was on vibrate, he probably didn't even know she had it. And he wouldn't feel a need to check. Constantly under his watchful eye, she wouldn't have an opportunity to use it. Even if she did somehow manage to call 9-1-1, she wouldn't be able to speak.

The hope that had sprung up flickered and died

as thoroughly as a candle in one of central Florida's downpours. The phone may as well be a Nintendo Game Boy for all the good it was going to do her.

Greg stepped back to study her, then raised the camera to take another picture. "That's a start. But we've definitely got some work to do."

When he approached her again, she braced herself for the second blow. It didn't help. Her head slammed backward into the tree and pain exploded across her mind. Almost immediately the side of her lower lip filled with heat and started to swell against the tape. Blood seeped into her mouth, warm and coppery. Clouds drifted over the moon and her vision blurred.

He moved away to amble back and forth in front of her, posture relaxed. "Don't worry about the appointment tomorrow evening. I'll be happy to keep it."

She blinked several times, trying to clear her thoughts. His words made little sense. She was floating on a sea of pain, her mind refusing to grasp the simplest concept. Appointment? What was he talking about?

A name rose to the surface and she cringed. Ashley Rittman. She had secured the appointment and then given Greg everything, right down to her home address. But Greg couldn't hurt Ashley. If he did, all fingers would be pointed at him.

"It would have been easier if I could have convinced Tomlinson to let you do it. As it stands, I'm supposed to be going along with Ford. But I'll figure something out. The department will be reeling with the news of your death. No one will think anything about the eager newbie heading off alone, determined to solve the case. I'll make sure I leave thirty minutes early. I'll even bring back all of Ashley's old pictures…after I remove the ones featuring a pink tutu." He stopped pacing to glare down at her. "Do you have any idea how humiliating that was? No, of course you don't. You beautiful, spoiled, popular women who play your games and watch the guys flock to you. Then when we're totally drawn in, you throw us away without any regard for how you've ruined our lives."

Lexi stared up at him, trying to follow his train of thought. Who was he talking about? Lysandra and her friends? Or the girlfriend who dumped him three years ago? Was that what triggered his need for revenge?

He clenched and unclenched his hands several times, cold fury running just beneath the surface. "Trust me, it was humiliating. But you got a real kick out of it, didn't you? You just had to mention that pink tutu in briefing and hear the snickers go around the room. Ten years later and I'm still being laughed at. But now it's your turn."

He snapped another picture and studied the display. He would probably be happy with the result. Already her left cheek was beginning to swell. She could feel it every time she blinked.

Finally he let the camera dangle against his chest. "Those beauty-queen looks of yours are fading fast. This is much more satisfying."

He moved closer and her heart began to pound. Although she tried to twist away, the third blow landed solidly on her right cheek, sending renewed pain flooding through her. Darkness encroached from all sides, creeping inward before once again retreating.

Greg pulled something from his back pocket and eased to the ground in front of her. He would wait long enough for the redness and swelling to appear, maybe even some bruising. Then he would take another picture and hit her again. He wasn't in any hurry. He had all night.

And hopefully he would take it. The longer he stretched out the ordeal, the greater the chance that Alan and the others would find her.

She closed her eyes and let the image of Alan's face fill her mind: his warm blue eyes, his teasing smile. Except now he wouldn't be smiling. He would be driving around, handsome face contorted with worry.

And praying. Yes, he would be doing a lot of praying. The thought gave her a small measure of peace, and for the first time, she understood the comfort that Alan seemed to get from his faith.

God, please. I'm not ready to die tonight. Please send help.

Greg spoke again, his words cutting across her thoughts. "This will give us the best picture of all."

He picked up the item he had removed from his pocket and her blood froze in her veins. It was a coiled bungee cord, one of those black rubber ones.

He unrolled it and gripped the two ends, stretching and releasing it as he talked.

"These final pictures are the most fun. Really unflattering. Have you ever seen anyone being strangled? Their face turns red, their eyes bug out—"

A rustle sounded nearby and he stopped midsentence, growing suddenly stiff with tension. It was probably just an armadillo or a possum. But after a dog had led someone to his last potential victim, Greg didn't appear ready to take a chance.

He dropped the bungee cord and pulled a pistol from an ankle holster before pushing himself to his feet. He hadn't used the gun the last time and probably regretted it. He could have killed the old man then finished off Denise and not left a live witness.

But killing the old man would have involved killing the dog, something she now knew Greg would never do. With his concern over Wendell's dog, she should have made the connection.

"Don't go anywhere." He gave her a cheeky grin, obviously not considering escape a possibility.

He was underestimating her. As soon as he was out of sight, she pulled her legs up and shifted her weight onto her knees. There was nothing she could do about her hands being tied. But if she could break free of the bindings on her legs, she would stand a chance.

She arched her back and gripped the rope, pulling hard to rotate the knot to the back, praying all the while. Once she had the knot where she could access it, she worked with shaking fingers, picking, pulling and grimacing as one then another nail broke off at the quick. Every rustle, every snap of a twig, sent panic spiraling through her. Greg was nearby, slipping silently between the trees, making sure they were alone. At any moment he would return and finish her off.

The last of the knot loosened and came free. She struggled to her feet and stumbled through the underbrush, feet catching on vines that threatened to topple her onto her face. She had no idea which way safety lay. She didn't care, as long as each step carried her farther from Greg.

Moments later, Greg's voice carried to her through the woods, taunting, almost playful.

"Oh, Lysandra, where are you?"

She froze in her tracks. If he heard her, he would be on her in moments. She couldn't run full speed with her hands tied behind her back. In fact, she couldn't do much more than a slow jog.

She pressed herself against a tree, her hands trapped between its rough bark and the phone in her back pocket.

Her phone.

She couldn't say anything. But if she called 9-1-1, they could use the phone's GPS to lock in her location.

She slid it from her pocket and twisted to the side, pulling her hands into view. She could see the screen, just barely. So she could dial 9-1-1.

It may not work, but she had to try.

It was her only hope.

SEVENTEEN

Alan crept slowly down Berkley Road, scouring its edge for a vehicle tucked in against the trees. He was coming up on the last wooded area before Polk City. And so far he had found nothing. Although her neighborhood was off of Berkley, it was just one of many possibilities. The thought left him struggling to push back hopelessness.

Lord, please lead us to the right place.

He had talked to Tomlinson again. Units had already been dispatched from Polk County, Winter Haven and Auburndale. And Polk County was working on getting a chopper in the air. But it was dark. One lone Jeep or Camry would be hard to spot. It would be much easier in the daylight.

Unfortunately, by daylight Lexi would be dead.

That sense of hopelessness descended again, this time with a vengeance. *Lord, please protect her. Please don't let her die.*

He scanned the roadside next to him, making frequent glances in the rearview mirror. Headlights approached, quickly closing the gap, and he tensed. As the car came closer without any signs of slowing down, he tapped the brakes and veered off the road. The driver blew the horn and swerved around him, with the passenger hanging out the window yelling obscenities.

Stupid kids. If they didn't slow down, they were going to get someone killed. They needed to be stopped and ticketed.

But not by him. And not tonight. Not only because he was in his Mustang—nothing was going to distract him from his search for Lexi.

As he prepared to ease back onto the road, the ringtone sounded on his phone. He tapped the Bluetooth, his pulse picking up speed. Lexi had her phone. Maybe she'd had a chance to use it.

With the first word out of the caller's mouth, disappointment collided with anticipation. It was Tomlinson. He apparently had news. Hopefully it was good.

"You got something?"

"She called."

His heart was pounding in earnest now. "Go ahead."

"She didn't say anything, but the call came from her phone. They've tracked the signal to an area off Recker Highway. There's a big wooded section near where that new extension of Main Street loops around."

"I'm headed there now."

He cut the wheels sharp left and stomped on the gas. Tires spun in the grass before catching and catapulting him onto the pavement then off the other side. Once his frantic U-turn was completed, he floored the accelerator and flew down the road, engine roaring. He knew the area Tomlinson mentioned. If he remembered right, just south of Main, a service road cut off Recker and went back into the woods. He could be there in seven or eight minutes. Five if he really pushed it.

Shortly after turning onto Recker Highway, an Auburndale police cruiser flew past him, lights flashing and siren screaming. By the time he reached the service road, more law enforcement had arrived, a sheriff's deputy and another Auburndale officer, and the sirens had been silenced. A closed gate spanned the entrance, a chain looped around the post. Closer inspection showed the chain had been cut.

One of the officers pushed open the gate and the three cruisers sped down the dirt road, engulfed in a cloud of dust. Alan followed. When they came to a stop, relief swept through him. Just off the road against the woods was a vehicle. A green Jeep.

Greg's green Jeep.

Alan approached the others. "We need to spread out and comb every square inch of these woods. More units will be arriving to give us a hand."

The sheriff's deputy stepped forward. "I can head that up. I hear she's one of ours."

Alan squinted at the nameplate. Sergeant Bailey. He was older, probably mid-fifties, and carried himself with an air of confidence that Alan found reassuring.

Yes, she was one of theirs. So was Greg.

Within minutes more law enforcement had arrived, and Sergeant Bailey had divided them up and given them each sections of the large wooded area.

As Alan jogged down the dirt road toward his assigned location, he listened for movement. Greg was likely close. He didn't leave his victims so deep in the woods that they couldn't be found. In fact, he wanted them to be found. It was all part of his plan to humiliate them the same way he had been humiliated.

Alan reached the bend that Bailey had pointed out on his map, clicked on the flashlight and headed in.

The undergrowth was thick. Florida's winters were too mild to kill the saplings, scrub and vines that occupied any natural areas. The tangled greenery hampered his movement and made stealth impossible. But he kept his flashlight beam aimed low and focused on trying not to sound like a Sasquatch lumbering through the woods.

Every minute or so he stopped to listen. If he couldn't move silently, neither could Greg. Or Lexi. The fact that she had been able to place that phone call made him believe that she had somehow escaped, at least temporarily. He clung to the hope that she was somewhere out there hiding while Greg searched.

Lord, please let us find her first.

A voice drifted to him, barely audible over the

rustle of his own footsteps. He froze in place. The air was still, whatever nightlife the forest possessed hunkered down in silence. It was as if all of nature was holding its breath. Had he imagined what he'd thought he heard?

He had just lifted a foot to take another step when it came again. No, he hadn't imagined it. It was a male voice, higher pitched. He held his breath and listened.

"Oh, Lysandra. Where are you?"

Hope surged through him. What he heard confirmed two things—Lexi was alive and she had escaped.

He flew into action, pushing himself forward, ignoring the vines and brambles that clawed at him as he passed.

"Oh, Lysandra." The voice was closer now. "Where are you?"

The singsong tone sent goose bumps sweeping over him. To Greg it was all a game. Lexi's life meant nothing.

Of course, he already knew that. Nothing meant anything to Greg except his perverted sense of justice.

The call came again, even closer. He was gaining on him.

"Lysandra, we're not finished yet. We still have one more photo to take."

Dread came crashing down on him, panic on its heels.

One more photo.

He knew all about that photo. He had seen it with each of the other victims.

That final photo wouldn't be taken until after she was dead.

Lexi stood motionless, dragging in ragged breaths and trying to stem the panic rising inside. She couldn't decide whether to stay where she was or run.

"Come here, Lysandra. It's time for the last picture."

He was moving closer. She was sure of it.

"You're not laughing now, are you? You had your fun at my expense, and now the tables are turned. It's not so funny being on the receiving end, is it?"

She took in some more ragged breaths, eyes wide, every muscle coiled and ready to spring.

"Where are you? Ready or not, here I come."

Greg continued his taunts, enjoying his macabre game of hide-and-seek. They filled the air around her, the embodiment of evil, chilling her from the outside in. She pressed herself more tightly against the tree, longing to shut out the words and the demented pleasure behind them.

But there was another sound, faint and deep—the distant rumbling of a helicopter. Her heart stuttered as relief washed through her, almost dropping her to her knees. Her frantic 9-1-1 call had gotten through. They were coming for her.

Then another thought flashed through her mind, wiping away that brief sense of relief. The chopper in the air didn't mean anything. Alan knew Greg had taken her. And he would have called Tomlinson. Of course they would utilize all their resources, not only to save her life but to put a permanent end to the killing. The chopper was searching, just like everyone on the ground. And with dozens of square miles of woods in the county, the chances of finding her in the dark were slim to none.

She leaned around the tree to look behind her. A light flashed through the trees, sweeping back and forth. Greg had his flashlight and he was headed her way.

The panic she had struggled to keep at bay exploded and she stumbled from her hiding place. Moments later, heavy footsteps sounded behind her, moving ever closer. She emerged in a clearing and, with an unobstructed path in front of her, broke into a full run. But there was no way she could escape him with her hands tied behind her back. And there was nowhere to hide.

Before she reached the middle of the clearing, he grabbed her by the shoulders and forced her to her knees. The next instant the cord was around her neck, squeezing more and more tightly. She twisted and bucked and even slammed her head into Greg's chest, but nothing she tried broke the hold he had on her. She sucked in one final breath through a mostly constricted airway before it was cut off completely.

She was going to die. She had her whole life ahead of her, a life that was to include Alan, but she was going to die. Why hadn't she listened? Why did she have to be so hardheaded? *Forgive me, sweetheart.*

But Alan's wasn't the only forgiveness she needed. All her life she had ignored God and pursued her own way with sheer stubbornness and determination. And look where it had gotten her.

Lexi cast her gaze heavenward. *Forgive me.*

The edges of her vision darkened, her angle of sight growing narrower and narrower. Soon she would black out, and it would all be over. Her ears filled with the throbbing of her own heart, then settled into a faint ring and finally a rumble that grew louder and louder until she could feel it in her chest. A wide beam of light circled the clearing. The cord suddenly loosened and fell from her neck, and she gulped in several frantic breaths.

The rumble was deafening now, the light blinding. It surrounded her, bathing her in virtual daylight.

The chopper. They had found her. Alan would be somewhere nearby.

Relief flooded her, mixed with a sort of euphoria. *Thank You, Lord.* She would never take anything for granted again. And she would give credit where credit was due. *Thank You, thank You, thank You.*

Greg hauled her to her feet and began to drag her toward the woods.

No! She wasn't going back into the woods. She had to stay where they could see her. Already the chopper was descending. The door swung open and a commanding voice came to them through a megaphone.

"Stay where you are. You're surrounded."

Greg ignored the command and continued to drag her toward the woods. She stomped hard on his instep then kicked at his knee. The first blow met with a grunt and curse. The second he twisted and deflected.

Neither seemed to slow him down. He bent and threw her over his shoulder as effortlessly as he would toss around a sack of potatoes. Ten more feet and they would disappear into the woods.

She reared back and twisted, hoping to throw him off balance. As she lifted her head, a figure emerged from the tree line behind them and ran forward, weapon drawn.

"Freeze."

It was Alan. Relief washed over her. But it didn't last long. Greg spun, pulled his pistol from the back of his waistband and fired off two shots. A scream rose up her throat, muffled by the tape. But Alan dropped and rolled and came out unscathed.

Another officer emerged from the woods. And another and another. Several more burst into the clearing from various points. They really were surrounded.

"Give it up, Greg." The words were Alan's. "Half of Polk County's police force is in these woods right now."

Greg hesitated for only a moment, then threw Lexi roughly to the ground. She somewhat broke her fall with one foot and landed hard on her side. Pain shot through her shoulder and a muffled groan made its way up her throat. She watched Greg throw down his

weapon and sprint the final feet toward the woods.
But before he could disappear from view, a law-enforcement officer charged into the clearing and wres-
tled him to the ground. Two deputies joined the fray.

She didn't see what happened next. Because suddenly Alan was on his knees beside her, wrapping
her in his arms and peppering her face with kisses.
He lifted her onto his lap and whispered her name
again and again, interspersed with I-love-yous and
more kisses. Finally he pulled away and reached for
the tape.

"I'm sorry. This is going to sting."

He ripped it loose with a grimace, then studied her
in the moonlight. When he lifted his hand to stroke
her cheek, his touch was gentle, but there was a tick
in his jaw and a hardness in his gaze. "He hurt you."

She attempted a weak smile. "I'm all right."

Yes, she was fine. Better than fine. Alan was holding her and Greg was in custody. The nightmare was
over. It could have been so much worse.

"If you guys hadn't gotten here when you did..."
A shudder shook her shoulders. "He had the cord
around my neck and..."

Alan didn't let her finish the thought. He pulled
her into a crushing embrace and claimed her mouth
with his own. Then he was kissing her cheeks and her
forehead and her hair and mumbling about how he
was never going to let her out of his sight again. She
buried her face in his muscular chest and breathed in
his clean, fresh scent.

Finally she pulled away to look up at him with a teasing smile. "Would you mind untying me, please? Unless you think I'm easier to control tied up."

He laughed, all the tension and worry and fear draining from him, then stood and pulled her to her feet. Once finished, he turned her to face him, holding both of her hands in his.

"I don't ever want to try to control you. I love you and respect you too much to try to turn you into something you're not."

"In this case, I should have listened to you. And I'm sorry. I almost got myself killed." She offered him another smile. "Thanks for having my back. I owe you my life."

"I'll always have your back. Forever, if you'll let me."

Forever? As in the rest of her life? Her eyes sought his, searching for the meaning behind his words.

Before he could say anything further, a figure came into her peripheral vision, and she turned to see Tomlinson running toward her. Judging from the ground he was covering, the younger cops didn't have anything on him. As soon as he reached her, he grasped both of her shoulders. Deep lines of worry marked his face, making him look ten years older.

"Are you all right?"

"I am now." She drew in a shaky breath. "I still can't believe it was Greg."

Tomlinson frowned. "Me, neither. I totally had him pegged wrong. He just seemed like a rookie cop, a little unsure of himself, but with all the zeal of a newbie."

Lexi nodded. "Now, in retrospect, it all makes sense. He was so focused on justice. Several times when we were working together he made comments that that's why we do what we do and why he became a cop. And he used that position to mete out his perverted form of justice."

A sudden chill swept over her in spite of the balmy night, and Alan draped an arm across her shoulders. She snuggled into his warmth, letting some of that masculine strength buoy her.

Tomlinson heaved a sigh. "But why now? Why lay low for almost ten years, then suddenly decide he needed revenge?"

Her gaze shifted to three figures crossing the clearing, two uniformed deputies with a slouched, shuffling Greg between them. His hands were cuffed behind his back and his head hung low. He would be going away for a long time, and would possibly even get the death penalty.

Pity stirred inside, unexpected and unwanted, but there all the same. Had he always been made fun of? Was he that skinny, geeky kid on the playground that the others tormented, the last one chosen for the team, always put down, always alone?

Her eyes again met Tomlinson's. "I don't know. But the day we picked up Wendell Moorehead, Greg mentioned that his girlfriend dumped him three years ago. Maybe that's what triggered all this. Maybe he got tired of feeling powerless and decided to take control. The timing is right. That would have been about when he started his police training."

Tomlinson shook his head. "I'm still having a hard time coming to terms with this."

His frown deepened. So did the furrows marking his face. He obviously liked Greg. Some of his angst was probably due to the fact that the killer had been right under his nose and he hadn't seen it. But he'd been right under all of their noses.

She grasped his hand and gave it a quick squeeze. "Don't beat yourself up. I worked with him, too, more closely than you did. And I didn't see it. I was so focused on someone *impersonating* a cop. I never once considered that it could be someone who *was* a cop. It's all so clear now."

Some of the tension left Tomlinson's features, and he gave her the first hint of a smile she had seen since he arrived. "You know what they say—hindsight is always twenty-twenty." He tilted his head to the right. "There's an ambulance waiting if you want to go to the hospital. It might not be a bad idea to get checked out. We'll take your report tomorrow."

She turned in the direction Tomlinson had indicated. She couldn't see anything through the trees, but the ambulance was probably sitting silently alongside the road, lights flashing. Fatigue washed over her, bone-numbing weariness at the thought of extending the night another two or three hours.

"No, I'm all right. I just want Alan to take me home."

"Okay. Take your time coming in tomorrow. I don't want to see you before noon."

"No argument there." She turned tired eyes up to Alan. His protective arm across her shoulder hadn't moved during the entire exchange with Tomlinson. Now he used it to direct her into the woods and toward his car.

As she settled into the leather bucket seat, she closed her eyes and let her head fall back. She would probably be asleep before they reached the outskirts of… She didn't even know where she was.

But Alan knew. He was going to take care of her, and that was all that mattered.

As sleep marched ever closer, she struggled to hold it back. They had a lot of talking to do. If not tonight, then soon. They were finished working together, at least professionally. But they had decisions to make. And a lot of years to regain. They needed to assess. And decide where to go next.

She needed to tell him she loved him.

And find out what he meant by forever.

EIGHTEEN

Lexi drew in a fragrant breath, soaking in the peace and tranquility that Harmony Grove's park offered. Alan's hand tightened around hers in a confirming squeeze. He apparently felt it, too. No one could ignore the beauty of nature's late-afternoon show.

The sun was finishing its descent, painting the sky in broad strokes of orange, gold and lavender. The glasslike surface of the lake reflected the fiery display. Tiny fish created ever-widening ripples, snacking on the water bugs lighting there, and a pair of mallard ducks moved silently along the water's edge. Darkness would fall soon, but the promise of impending night no longer held an unspoken threat.

Alan gave her hand another squeeze. "Are you doing all right?"

"I'm okay." She smiled up at him. Ever since the previous evening, he had been so attentive. Even more than usual.

The terror of last night was still fresh in her mind, but a good night's sleep had done wonders. She had gone in to the station and taken care of her reports. She had even stopped by her mom's house to throw a load of clothes in the wash and been surprised to find one already spinning in the dryer. Her ankle was still wrapped, and the crutches were within easy reach, but she was actually up doing something for herself.

Lexi had mentally prepared for the pity party, the subtle control tactics. But they never came. Instead, her mom greeted her with a smile and a hug. For the first time ever, she seemed to look on her as an independent adult, with a life separate from her own. Maybe it had something to do with almost losing her. Or maybe she had finally come to the conclusion that trying to control her was a colossal waste of time. Whatever her reasons, Lexi was more inclined to just accept rather than question the gift.

Yes, she was doing well. After leaving her mother's house, she had met Alan for a romantic dinner out. Now she was content, in love and pleasantly full.

Alan drew to a stop in front of a wooden bench overlooking the lake. "How about a break?"

A break sounded good. So did a walk. Any activity had appeal as long as she was with Alan. She sank onto the wooden slats next to him and rested her head against his shoulder.

He drew in a deep breath. "When I realized that Greg was the killer and that he had taken you, I was so afraid I had lost you. I can't tell you what I felt in those moments."

"I know. I always try to be optimistic and never give up, but I have to confess, there were several times I was pretty sure I was a goner."

He released her hand to wrap an arm around her and pull her closer still. "I love you, Lexi. I don't ever want to let you go. But I don't want to smother you, either. And I never want to try to control you."

"I love you, too. And right now, a little bit of smothering doesn't sound so bad."

For several minutes they sat in silence, watching the colors leech out as the final remnants of day faded.

"Do you know what's significant about this spot?" Alan's tone held a hint of teasing.

"This is where you first kissed me." She grinned over at him. "Remember, *I'm* the one who told *you*. You had forgotten."

"But I remember it well now. The full moon, the stars spread across the sky, the few straggling couples who weren't ready to call it a night and go home."

Warmth spread through her chest, bringing with it a smile. He remembered more than she thought he had.

"I wondered what you would do if I kissed you. I was afraid I might be rushing things. But if I remember right, you were quite receptive."

Yes, his memory had served him well. They had been dating for two weeks, and she was beginning to think he would never kiss her.

He released a contented sigh. "This is definitely a special place. But I think it needs some more significance."

More significant than their first kiss? How was he going to manage that? She leaned away to look over at him. He was smiling, his gaze warm. Her heart skipped a beat.

"When I told you I would have your back forever if you'd let me, I meant it."

He took both of her hands in his, and her heart began to pound. When he slid off the bench to drop to one knee, it almost stopped.

"Lexi, I'd like to ask you to marry me. If you're not ready, I can wait. I've waited for six years. What's another few months?"

Her mind whirled. He was asking her to marry him. Emotion flooded her, love for this man who devoted his life to serving others, who cared so deeply it hurt, who put her on a pedestal and kept her there. He had asked once, and she had blown it. Giving up her independence had seemed too big of a price to pay.

Now she was getting a second chance. No, she didn't want to wait.

She dropped to her knees in front of him and wrapped both arms around his neck. "After six long years, I think we've waited long enough. I'll marry you tomorrow if you want."

He pulled her to him in a crushing hug and laughed, his breath warm in her hair. "You might need a little longer than that to plan a wedding."

"Okay, two weeks."

He stood, lifted her off the ground and spun her around. Giddiness swept through her, and her laughter spilled out, carried away on the gentle night breeze. She was marrying Alan. And she was doing it without hesitation or regret. So what if she was giving up a small piece of her independence? So was he.

He set her back on her feet and began a replay of that long-ago kiss. But this one held all the pent-up emotion of six years of longing.

And she was sure she saw some of those Memorial Day fireworks that preceded the first kiss. She melted into his arms and surrendered completely.

Independence for love. A good trade, indeed.

* * * * *

Dear Reader,

I hope you enjoyed reading Lexi and Alan's story. Lexi took a tragedy in her life, the murder of her best friend, and let it spur her to pursue justice for others. But she had also allowed the bad things in her life to keep her from a relationship with God. Once she stopped blaming God, she began to see Him as a loving Heavenly Father. Alan had made some bad decisions in the past, but then committed from that point on to rely on God to direct his path. His faith was the real deal and showed in his kindness and concern for those he served.

Alan found forgiveness for his past mistakes and a fresh start, but Lysandra was tormented by guilt over her part in unwittingly creating a killer. Although most of us haven't done anything to cause another person's death, we've all made decisions or done things that we regret and may be "kicking ourselves." It's nice to know that God doesn't hold those past mistakes against us when we confess them to Him. Psalm 103:12 says, "As far as the east is from the west, so far has He removed our transgressions from us." My prayer is that, if you are struggling with feelings of guilt and regret, you will find the release and freedom that only God can give.

Thank you for reading *Out for Justice*. For more information about me and my books, check out my website at www.caroljpost.com. You can find me on

Facebook at www.facebook.com/CarolJPost.Author, or drop me a line at caroljpost@gmail.com. I love to connect with readers!

May God richly bless you.
Carol J. Post

Questions for Discussion

1. Alan remembered the younger Lexi as being sweet and compliant, with an innocence about her, but the knocks of life had given her a bit of a hard edge. Were you able to relate to her? Why or why not?

2. Alan was very kindhearted. It showed in the way he treated Lexi, in his concern for troubled youth, even in his willingness to marry Lauren and care for her child when he believed he had lost Lexi. Did you like him as a hero? Why or why not?

3. Lexi always had a soft spot in her heart for animals and, as a result, ended up with three cats. How about you? Do you find it hard to turn away an animal in need? How many pets do you have?

4. When Lexi's best friend was murdered several years earlier, she changed her career plans from something business-related to law enforcement. What events in your life have shaped your career choices?

5. Lexi and Alan learned that Lexi's mother's lies had changed the course of their lives. What could they have done differently at the time? How do you think things would have turned out for them if they had taken a different course?

6. Lexi blamed God for taking her best friend, then her father and finally her cousin Kayla. How can you reach people who are having a hard time seeing God as a loving Heavenly Father because of all the bad they have experienced in their lives?

7. Although hazing has been illegal for years, it still goes on at many colleges across the country. Do you believe that university officials are doing enough to stop it? What other actions can be taken?

8. After losing Lexi then going through a bad marriage, Alan hit bottom and finally reached out to God. What events have been turning points in your life?

9. Lexi was afraid of commitment, in part because her parents had a poor marriage. Were your parents good or bad examples of what a marriage should be? Were there other people in your life who modeled a godly marriage?

10. Lexi's mother had unfulfilled dreams and tried to project those onto Lexi. Have you seen examples of this? How were the children affected?

11. When Alan believed that Lexi had found someone else, he married Lauren on the rebound and ended up regretting his rash decision. What are some

good principles one can follow to avoid making poor decisions?

12. Alan and Lexi had to set aside their differences and work together. Have you ever been stuck in an uncomfortable working relationship with someone? How did you handle it? Did things eventually get better, or did one or the other of you leave?

13. Alan had a heart for troubled youth and tried to help steer Duncan in the right direction. What are some ways we can be a positive influence on teens heading down the wrong track?

14. When Lexi was upset, she often found comfort in playing the piano. What activities help you re-group and find peace?

15. Were you surprised to learn the identity of the killer? At what point did you know?

LARGER-PRINT BOOKS!

GET 2 FREE LARGER-PRINT NOVELS PLUS 2 FREE MYSTERY GIFTS

Love Inspired

Larger-print novels are now available...

ReaderService.com

Manage your account online!

- Review your order history
- Manage your payments
- Update your address

*We've designed
the Harlequin® Reader Service
website just for you.*

Enjoy all the features!

- Reader excerpts from any series
- Respond to mailings and
  special monthly offers
- Discover new series available to you
- Browse the Bonus Bucks catalog
- Share your feedback

Visit us at:
ReaderService.com